About the Author

Mark Macrossan grew up in Brisbane. Previous occupations include barrister (Sydney) and film extra (London). He currently lives in Sydney.

The Volcanologist is his second novel.

He can be found online at www.markmacrossan.com.

THE VOLCANOLOGIST

Mark Macrossan

ANTIMERIDIAN

The Volcanologist

Prologue

THE SOLDIER, when we stumble upon him, is illuminated by the sunrise and he's glowing, almost ablaze, as if he's some sort of biblical apparition. He's lying on his back at an altitude of 4,300 metres, just below the summit of the mountain – a volcano, in fact – and he's staring out over the jungle far below and towards the distant Congolese hills. His open eyes, though, are blank, unmoved by the view, oblivious to the swirling mists. Not at peace exactly, but resigned, in a permanent state of surrender.

Not that there was a choice apparently. Death would have been quick by the looks of things: a bullet through the heart – a bullet which is now embedded somewhere in the soil beneath the surrounding clumps of tussock grass and lichen. We note the spent AK-47 cartridges scattered around like spilled treasure, and I stand there for a while as the others continue to search the area.

I'm still standing there when it hits me like a train.

Dala.

Δ

The next day, back in Goma, I find myself looking up at a policewoman in a black beret. Looking up, I might add, in a dishevelled kind of way. The policewoman, whose name I've already gathered is Officer Kitenge, pronounced *Kit-engi* with a hard 'g', is reading notes of some kind. Officer Kitenge is tall, thin, dark and mean.

Her fellow officer, Mwepu, walks in. Mwepu clearly hasn't shaved.

'Where's your cap?' she asks.

Mwepu shrugs. 'Lost it.'

'You *lost* it?' She shakes her head in disbelief and goes back to her notes.

I am, as I say, looking a bit rough at this point and despite my circumstances, I'm conscious of how creased and dirty my jacket and trousers have become. It's strange, I reflect, the things that can occur to a person in these situations. I look at Mwepu, pleadingly – it's a long shot, but worth a try. Mwepu, however, shows no sympathy, avoids my stare, and sits down, keeping his distance from everyone else. Mwepu, who has red-rimmed watery eyes, appears to be of little use to anyone. Only good for losing things.

And then the penny drops. The *cap*. Mwepu's missing beret.

Officer Kitenge looks up from her notes again and stares at me with her merciless dark eyes. Black eyes, they're even blacker than her skin, which is the blackest skin I've ever seen. Her eyes are like polished obsidian – beautiful, perhaps, in different circumstances – and I can see my reflection in them.

'What is your occupation?'

This being the DRC – the Democratic Republic of Congo – everyone's speaking in French. Which isn't a problem for me, although I'm beginning to wish it was. Or at least, I'm beginning to wish I'd *said* it was.

'I'm a volcanologist,' I reply.

Which makes the policewoman laugh. Maybe she has a sense of humour after all, I think. The levity, however, vanishes as quickly as it appears.

'Of course. Except that doesn't fully explain what you were doing on a volcano that's been inactive for *ten thousand years*.'

She has a point, and I'm too tired to argue. Instead, I notice how dirty the floor is, how it could do with a polish, or at least a simple mopping. I look more closely at the dirt and wonder if it's blood and pray it isn't. It could be mud. Mud or blood.

'Perhaps less a volcanologist,' she continues, 'and more a soldier. A soldier of fortune. A mercenary.'

'Absolutely not.'

'A Russian mercenary.'

'No. One hundred percent no. I'm—'

'You're Russian.'

'No, I'm…' I hesitate, a natural cautiousness, but obviously ill-advised in this kind of situation. 'I'm British.'

'British!' She laughs again, and seems to find this even funnier than my stated occupation. 'A British volcanologist. Then how do you explain what we found in your pocket?'

Another good point. I'm thinking: how *do* I explain that?

'What was that name again?' she says to Mwepu. 'The name he's been using?'

Mwepu fumbles about with some papers and hands her a single sheet that looks like a photocopy of something.

'So according to you,' she says to me, reading the document, 'you are…' She has trouble and shows it to Mwepu. 'What does that say?'

To no-one's surprise, Mwepu can't assist. So I step in.

Or I'm about to.

But again, I hesitate. Because I know that significant consequences may well flow from these answers. If it isn't too late. If they haven't already made up their minds who I am.

But have I, though? Have I made up my mind who I am?

Δ

The short answer is I'm John Penne.

Most of the time.

I was once an intelligence officer with the SIS, the British secret service. And still would be, if they'd have had me back. No chance now.

And that really sums me up. Everything else in my life has been such a tangle of contradiction, I really don't think I know who I am anymore. If I ever did.

I've always been a bit directionless, I suppose – clutching for an identity, you might say. Trying to find my place in the world. Many might regard the secret service – the job of a spy, in other words – as being patently the wrong fit for a man trying to find his true identity, but then again, you could equally regard it as being the perfect home for someone without a strong sense of self.

There's one more thing I can say about myself (last but certainly not least): I once fell in love with a woman who didn't love me back. Or maybe she did. But either way, as things have turned out, meeting her has proven to be a significant danger to my health. To put it mildly.

If I had the power to turn back the clock, would I do things differently? The obvious response is yes, I would. I'm not insane. But the funny thing is, I can't help but think there's a side of me, given the chance, given a reprieve, that would do the same thing all over again. Even knowing where it leads. Now there's a disturbing thought.

This story is the story of 'us', of me and her. I have to warn you, it's a bit of a travelogue – a *volcanologue* might be a fitting name for it. But whatever you want to call it, it's the only story I can tell you about myself that goes any way towards defining my life.

And from where I stand given the way events have unfolded – it could well be the last story I'll ever tell.

Δ

Inasmuch as any story has an unequivocal starting point, it all really began just over two years ago. Only two years, it's difficult to believe. It feels like a lifetime. People say that all the time, but in my case it's no exaggeration.

1.

SHE WAS only ever a blonde, back then.

Or at least as far I was concerned, she was. In my head.

From the start, I knew what she looked like because I had her photograph in my coat pocket and I'd looked at it many times; I'd been struck, from the first viewing, by her... well I was going to say by her singular prettiness, but pretty isn't the right word. I don't actually know what the right word is, it probably doesn't exist, but let's just say she was striking. Strikingly attractive.

It was April last year, and I was in Geneva. It was a crisp Tuesday morning, and I was enjoying my first coffee for the day in the central train station. It was just after Easter and the station was busy with holidaymakers: late-season skiers, tourists, families with children, friends with friends and lovers with lovers. And me. I was standing outside the ticket office because I'd received information that she'd be there, boarding a certain train to Paris, and I knew who to look for because, as I say, I had her photograph in my pocket.

Even back then though, I didn't need the photograph. Her image was perfectly and permanently preserved in my mind's eye: dark blonde hair that was almost brown, olive skin, blue-green eyes. Slightly Russian-looking, consistent with her family history. Thirty-one years old. Height, about 5' 7" or 5' 8", or just over 170cm, therefore not short. Slim. Determined, needed no-one. Least of all me.

In fact back then she needed me like a bad dose of swine flu, because I'd been instructed to haul her in. Not literally, that was never my job. My job, as a rule, was limited to research, field spotting and communications. In this instance, once I'd found and spotted the target, I was to notify a 'middleman' and continue to maintain a visual up until capture. This middleman – who I understood was in some way connected to the French secret service – would in turn alert the appropriate tactical response team to take care of the physical side of things. I was just a humble intelligence officer and contrary to the public perception, intelligence officers, as a rule at least, were never supposed to get their hands dirty. In this particular case though, I managed to do just that – for reasons that will be made clear – but that had never been the plan. After I'd tracked down and spotted the target, I had, in effect, just one simple job to do: make a phone call while continuing to maintain a visual.

One simple job and I blew it.

I should say that I didn't know all that much about what this target of mine was supposed to have done. I knew that an agent, 'one of ours' they told me – a female British asset who also happened to be a British citizen – had been killed somewhere in the Alps, her body ended up in a lake, and that the target and one other person had been implicated. She and her associate were allegedly DGSE operatives – members of the French secret service – and they'd supposedly 'gone rogue'. It was believed to have been a kidnapping gone wrong – possibly a botched attempt to extract information – and there was a suggestion that the rogue operatives may have been acting at the behest of an unidentified foreign power. The associate had disappeared and was possibly dead himself, but my target was still very much in the picture. In any event, I'd been told that due to 'matters of some sensitivity' this was to be kept out of the hands of the local homicide squad, but that the French and the Swiss were 'cooperating with us unconditionally for a change', which was supposed to have made the whole thing 'exponentially simpler'. A lovely word, 'exponentially'. All in all, the whole business was a perfect example of how life never turns out the way we expect it to. *Never.*

So there I was, standing outside the ticket office, sipping my coffee, waiting for her. I was confident she'd show, my informant had a good track record. I checked my watch: it was now a little under one hour before the next fast train to Paris, the one she was supposed to be catching. I'd already bought my ticket, it seemed like a safe enough bet.

I'd also been told she'd booked a flight – using a false name and passport, details unknown. The plane was due to depart Paris later that day for Kuala Lumpur, Malaysia, although she was unlikely to be leaving on it, or not that day at least: all flights had been grounded due to an ash cloud – *that* ash cloud – courtesy of an Icelandic volcano with an unpronounceable name. All of which, in any event, was supposedly academic: with any luck she'd be intercepted well before she got anywhere near the airport.

And she did eventually appear. That much went to plan, at least.

45 minutes before departure: I finally spotted her, walking briskly into the ticket office. Unmistakeable. Her stature and features matched perfectly the photograph in my pocket – and the one in my head. Her eyes alone – were they blue or were they green? – her eyes gave her away, even from where I stood. Today her shoulder-length blonde hair was spilling, and elegantly unruly. She was wearing fitted black jeans, a green jacket, and a beige scarf that almost matched her hair colour. And tan boots that clicked sharply across the concourse. The other thing I remember is she was carrying a small dark-brown shoulder bag.

The great thing about your target being an attractive female, is you can look at them openly without fear of raising a suspicion in them: they're used to being stared at by predictable, tedious men. Or women.

I managed to get close enough to hear her request a ticket

to Paris. I even caught the carriage number she was allocated: carriage 5, two away from mine.

Of course, I could have called her in then and there. (If only. How differently it all would have turned out. Everything, my life included.) But I had to ensure it wasn't a ruse. Apart from anything else, I wasn't going to be made a fool of. So my plan was to follow her onto the train first. Then and only then, all the while maintaining visual contact, would I make the call. I would continue to observe her right up until her capture, in case she got off before the team arrived. It was a solid plan. Not foolproof, but solid, and that's all you could ever ask for in a plan. So when she exited the ticket office, I followed her.

She browsed some kiosks, possibly looking for something to eat on the train.

35 minutes before departure: I lost her. One minute she was looking at pastries, the next she was gone. Had I simply been careless? Or had she sensed she was being followed? Or it could all have been a trick, the ruse I was trying to guard against. Perhaps she never had any intention of catching the train to Paris from the outset. I had little choice, though, other than to trust my information – my informant, after all, had been proven to be eminently trustworthy – so after quickly checking the street outside, I simply noted the time and headed for the departure platform.

23 minutes before departure: As I stood next to the Paris train on platform 8, a sharp whistle signified the imminent departure of the train behind me on platform 7. After it banged and creaked and began to move, I caught the passing array of tinted faces peering out – faces looking serious, happy, quizzical, but mostly content and self-absorbed, and all of them vanishing into the morning haze. I was reasonably confident, though, that hers wouldn't be among them, because it was the Zurich train. I had to assume she was still heading the other way, to Paris, to where she was hoping to board that flight to Southeast Asia.

19 minutes before departure: I found her again. To my great relief, I spotted her on the platform about twenty metres away, taking gulps of water from a plastic Evian bottle. I have no idea how she suddenly got there, but good spies have an ability to materialise like that, seemingly out of thin air. And disappear, too, obviously. I endeavoured to keep a closer eye on her this time. There was no sign she was trying to avoid a tail – as far as I could tell.

The water did make me wonder, though: nerves?

11 minutes before departure: With just over ten minutes to go, she turned on one heel, threw her plastic bottle in a rubbish bin and made for the female toilets. I had no choice but to stand guard outside. Time passed, agonizingly slowly, as I waited for her to re-emerge.

5 minutes before departure: She still hadn't come out. My pulse rate was up. Had I missed her? Was she already on the train? Or were my earlier fears well-founded, and was this all a ploy designed to put the dogs off their scent? To pack them off on a wild-goose chase? My gut instinct was telling me that she was going to Paris, but I had to guard against failure – I knew I had to stick to the plan and only board the train after I'd witnessed her doing the same.

I continued to carefully observe each and every person leaving the female toilets…

… A young woman with red hair came out carrying a bulging *Printemps* shopping bag. She was wearing a loud sixties dress and talking animatedly to an old woman, possibly her mother, perhaps post-shopping trip. The happy lives some people led!

… She was followed by a blonde woman in gym wear, maybe in her fifties, with her hair in a tight bun and carrying a sports bag.

… Another blonde came out. This one, shouldering a bag with a Danish flag sewn onto it, was rushing for the train and made my heart skip. She had the hair, and seemed the right age, but although I couldn't see her face, she was too plump. I watched as she disappeared into the clusters of passengers converging on the platform.

… Next in line was a thirty-something black woman in colourful clothes, nonchalantly dragging a small, wailing boy, mid-meltdown.

… Then a middle-aged brunette in a figure-hugging navy woollen dress, wheeling a small flight-attendant's suitcase and walking as if every man on the platform was staring at her. Not her, I would have staked my life on it.

… And the next one I could safely rule out too: a girl with short brown hair and pale skin, wearing a death metal t-shirt under a black leather jacket. She was joined by a similarly dressed male with a mohawk, two peas in a pod…

1 minute before departure. The whistle blew and there was still no sign of her. I almost weakened and boarded the train, but I stuck with the plan and resisted. Sometimes, I told myself, you had to exert some self-discipline and ignore your 'better instinct' – an instinct which was frequently nothing more than a subliminal urge to seek out the path of least resistance. After all, what was the point of having a plan?

The train began to move. With one eye still on the toilet entrance, I watched the procession of carriages and waited for number 5.

3… 4…

By the time carriage number 5 had reached me, the train had already begun to pick up speed. But it wasn't yet travelling too rapidly for me to notice, staring out one of the windows, the face of the redhaired woman in the sixties dress. I couldn't see if the old woman she'd been talking to was sitting with her, but you could bet your bottom dollar she wasn't, because this time, from this angle, I could clearly see the redhaired woman's face and there could be no doubt about it: it was the same face as the one in the photograph in my jacket pocket.

A wig and a change of clothes, I'd been fooled by the oldest trick in the book. Even the *Printemps* bag should have put me on notice: *Printemps* was a famous Parisian department store and there was no *Printemps* store in Geneva – it wasn't bulging from shopping, but from the dark-brown shoulder bag she'd been carrying when I first saw her.

How did I fall for it? Perhaps I'd been so captivated by her looks in the photograph that I was thrown by the smallest alteration in them. It was no excuse, but a reason.

So what to do? As I wasn't on the train, and had no visual on her, I wasn't able to call in the heavies.

Without calling in the big guns and risking another embarrassing mistake, what I *should* have done – it's obvious now – was to report in to my superiors. They could have got someone else onto it. I would have covered myself, admitting only to what was, let's face it, an easy mistake. And so why didn't I? Two reasons: first, I didn't want to admit my failure – *any* failure – if I didn't have to, and second, I was ambitious and hungry and wanted this one for myself. And perhaps, also, I was just a little possessive about her from the beginning.

Anyway, the way I saw it at the time, all was not lost. I was fairly certain she hadn't seen me, and that she'd been simply deploying a standard procedure to confuse any tails. So I could safely assume I'd retained the advantage of her not knowing who I was. I could assume she was still going to Paris and that she'd still be attempting to catch her flight to Malaysia, so I could continue my pursuit of her there. It was true that I wasn't able to jump on a plane and hope to get to Paris around the same time – the ash cloud made sure of that, there were no flights at all, anywhere, in this part of the world. But it was a double-edged sword and she was faced with the same impediment. Her flight would be delayed for at least a day if not days. I could redeem myself by catching the next train, it would only arrive two hours after hers.

All good in theory.

Who says hindsight is a wonderful thing? It's not wonderful as far as I'm concerned, it's a whole world of pain all on its own. Because what I hadn't counted on at the time, had I, was the lifting of the grounding order in Paris. The ash cloud had moved on – a fairly obvious possibility, more so with hindsight – and by the time I'd arrived at Charles de Gaulle airport in the late afternoon, my bird had flown the coop.

Δ

I blithely say 'my bird has flown the coop'. I evasively cling to 'she'. It's tempting, even now, to hold back from pinning a name to her. She's used so many different ones, and certainly back then no-one had any real fix on her, over and above what any background checks may have revealed. (Did that ever change?) Her childhood was a foggy mystery, but prior to becoming a DGSE operative, it appeared she'd worked as a model while studying journalism and later wrote an occasional column for a Parisian newspaper, writing under the name of 'Delphine G'.

She even had her own code name. After the Alps incident, she was referred to in the Service as SANDPIPER. Given sandpipers are migratory birds, the name turned out to be oddly appropriate (which was almost certainly unintentional, as code names are supposed to be more bland than apt). It clearly, though, won't do for present purposes.

Our best guess at the time was that her real name, her birth name, was Dala Gasnier. Indeed it appeared she may have had a Russian relative, a great aunt, with the same first name.

So let's just call her Dala, then, shall we?

2.

Thursday, 22 April
Grand Hyatt Hotel, Kuala Lumpur,
Malaysia

SHE MAY have moved on, but she'd left a presence that was tangible.

Night-time, two days later, I found myself on the other side of the world, sitting on a king-size bed in the Kuala Lumpur Grand Hyatt, looking out at the restless city. Beyond the park below and the adjacent twin towers, distant lights sparkled and winked at me, both inviting and shunning.

Dala had had a one-day head start. After getting off the train in Paris on Tuesday afternoon and heading straight for the airport, I was confronted with the chaos and confusion wreaked by the ash cloud, and despite the lifting of the grounding order, I had to wait until the following evening before I could board a plane and follow her.

And now I'd missed her again, but not by much. Discreet inquiries made with various hotel employees revealed that she'd checked out late, only a few hours ago. She'd caught a taxi, but they couldn't tell me where to.

Δ

It had been back in Paris, after the departure of Dala's flight, that I'd decided to finally spill the beans to my immediate superior, Alan. I can't describe the humiliation I felt in doing this – in attempting to explain how I first allowed the target to slip through my fingers in Geneva, why I hadn't immediately contacted him when this happened, and how I hadn't foreseen the lifting of the order grounding all flights. Alan, though – cold, cold Alan – did apparently have a heart buried deep beneath those many layers of glacial ice, and it was my good fortune, or so I thought at the time, that he now provided me with evidence of this fact.

I was phoning him from Charles de Gaulle airport. Dala's plane had taken off half an hour earlier, and the departures board across the concourse was taunting me in the background. I'd just told him *most* of what had happened – I decided to leave out the bit about the change of clothes and the red wig.

'So let me get this straight,' Alan was saying. Names were never used in these phone calls, but something told me Alan wasn't the type to use them anyway. He even avoided code names unless absolutely necessary. 'And I'm not even going to ask why you didn't just get on the train if you trusted your information. But then... despite visually verifying her departure on the TGV in Geneva, you nevertheless decided not to report that fact, due to—'

'Yup.'

He left a brutal pause before continuing.

'Due to your assessment that you would be able to safely... *safely* catch up with her in Paris.'

'That's correct.'

Another pause.

'In Paris, a city of... how many people?'

'About ten, these days I believe.'

'Ten million people.'

'Can I just say this, though, in my defence. Because I had her flight details, and because the ash—'

'How sure are you she was on that flight?' he asked.

'Well my information—'

'No visual confirmation?'

'No.'

'No documentary confirmation?'

Meaning, did I know what name she was travelling under?

'No.'

While Alan was thinking, I added:

'I can say this, though, my informant's record to date has been excellent.'

'That may well be.'

More thinking. Another thought occurred to me:

'Why don't we get our KL people to wait for her at the

other end? Pick her up when she gets off the plane?'

'No,' he said. 'We can't be sure it was her that you saw, or if it was, whether she boarded the plane. We don't even have a name – she'll undoubtedly be travelling under a false passport. No. I'm not going to risk an international incident, especially as our relationship with the Malaysians is, shall we say, a little fragile at present. Anyway, I want to keep this… in-house, as it were. Just between us.'

'Because of my stuff-up?'

'Partly. And for other reasons you needn't be troubled with at the moment.'

'Right.'

Another sigh, another pause.

'OK,' he said, finally. 'You fucked up – *colossally* fucked up – but all's not lost. This is recoverable. If you're absolutely certain it was her…'

'I am.'

'… and if we… how shall I put it?… unleash you… how confident are you that you'd be able to catch up with her again? It's a big place, Asia. Bigger than Paris.'

'I'm certain I would,' I lied. 'One hundred percent.'

The truth was that my information only related to her itinerary into Paris and out again. I doubted my informant would be able to come up with anything further, now that she'd left Europe. But I lied because, as I say, I was ambitious. And isn't that what every employer looks for in an employee?

Also, I'd never been to Asia. What better way to rectify

that than a trip there at Her Majesty's expense?

There was an even longer pause and I heard a sigh.

'Keep this close to your chest.' Alan wasn't exactly old school, but he did like the old clichés. 'Follow her. Find her. And when you do, report to no-one but me.'

'So no…?' I searched for the appropriate allusion; I was thinking of my previous instructions to call the French middleman.

'No. You continue to report to me and no-one else.'

It occurred to me that Alan was just doing what I'd been doing. Making sure if there was only one dessert to go around, he'd be the one to get it.

'And one last thing,' he continued. 'No more mistakes. This failure to report must never happen again, OK? *Ever.* That's the deal. You'll have my complete support, but that's the deal. Never again.'

And there you had it. The deal. Which was to prove to be another cog in the machinery of my undoing.

Δ

And as I sat there on that king-size bed in that unfamiliar city, it occurred to me that this could have been her room. That Dala could have been sitting on this very bed the night before, looking out at this very view.

I imagine her sitting there.

In one of the hotel's bathrobes, perhaps. Considering a shower – no, a bath – after the long flight. But first admiring

21

the twinkling colours of this bustling Asian city which, at this glassed-in, aerial remove at least, appeared almost equanimous and non-judgemental in its evening repose.

And then she's in the bathroom with its large white bathtub, and its floor to ceiling glass wall, a window to the rest of the world.

She slips off her robe and slides into the bath. She ducks underwater and re-emerges, her blonde head now as sleek as a seal's, and she glances out the window, the city lights reflected in her blue-green eyes.

I picture all of her. She has an admirable figure. Her body is both athletic and womanly: as hard as a diamond, and as soft as a kiss. She's a Greco-Roman statue come to life, polished marble with a heartbeat. She's a crime of Nature, given what she has and others don't.

And she's not just a picture of beauty, an object of male and female desire; she's clever too. I am certain of this without knowing exactly why.

Maybe I'm thinking about Dala's associate, her fellow DGSE operative who's since vanished. Whether this second person is still at large is a moot point, but Dala has at least been smart enough to travel alone. She knows what she's doing. Streetwise, at the very least.

She's certainly cunning enough to have made it, still free as a bird, to this five-star hotel in Kuala Lumpur, with its beautiful bath overlooking the muted city, and sitting there on that bed I can see her again in my mind's eye, surrounded by white shells and gardenia soap and pumice stone (the only rock that floats, is that her?), and telling herself how much better this is than a prison.

This was good, I told myself. The best way to catch someone is to put yourself in their shoes. Become them.

Looking back, though, it was more than that. It wasn't simply as a way of doing my job – of catching her – that I was attempting to see the world through her eyes. Something else, I suspect, had begun to tick over in that unconscious brain of mine. Something insidious.

3.

Monday, 26 April
Westin Resort, Langkawi Island,
Malaysia

SHE WAS still a day ahead of me, no more, no less.

Was she toying with me?

After Kuala Lumpur, I'd headed north, to the island of Langkawi, a pearl of a place, albeit somewhat developed, sitting fetchingly in the Strait of Malacca, adjacent to Malaysia's border with Thailand. I'd done this because I managed to score myself another tip-off, this time from Alan, so I couldn't claim any credit for it. But I'd done some detective work of my own and managed to track her down to the Westin resort there. But as was the case in KL, Dala had departed before I arrived, so I took some time out by the hotel pool to contemplate my next move.

The resort, situated on an attractive bay and with a view across turquoise waters to hilly green islands, was like large tropical resorts everywhere. They're all clones, and you know you shouldn't like them, but you just can't help yourself. With their sunken pool bars and twisting, palm-fringed walkways. And those all-you-can-eat international breakfasts, patronized by honeymooners and hangoverers alike, surely only the snobbiest of guests could find fault with them?

I was sitting on a deck chair, with just an infinity pool between me and the Malacca Strait. The pool, which was almost empty, contained just a couple of sunbathers cooling their sun-scorched skin. My skin, too, was becoming a little warm, well on its way to burning. Soon I'd have to jump in that pool myself. Meanwhile I continued to pretend to read an airport novel through dark sunglasses.

Unlike Dala, I didn't bother with disguises. My job certainly didn't, as a rule, require it. And anyway, as far as my looks went, they were nothing to write home about. I was no James Bond, and didn't pretend I was. Not the prettiest face in the Service, in other words, but that was fine by me. Bland was a bonus in my job.

Not that you'd call my looks *bland* exactly. At least I don't think so. If Dala had been handed a description of me, how would it have read? Age, 36. Light brown hair (more sandy, in my opinion, almost blond, and a little wavy, or 'unruly'), and hazel eyes (blue-green-brown, a bit of everything – I've been told I have 'kind eyes'.) Slim to athletic build (let's say 'toned', I work out). Height 5' 11" (180cm), weight 11 stone (154 pounds, or 70kg) (and, I should add, a body/mass index of 21.6, placing me bang in the middle of healthy, and making me dux of something at least).

With the right clothes and a better tan, I could pass for a professional surfer. Unlike most of my compatriots, I tan well, and in the right conditions burn as brown as an Arab camel-trader. Guess I must have some black Irish in me.

Actually I could pass for a lot of things, I've always slipped into roles fairly comfortably. I'm not sure why, perhaps it has something to do with my background. Only child, born in the north of England, accent bashed out of me at a posh boarding school in the south. Father was a solicitor (in more ways than one, I suspect) who left my mother when I was young. Or perhaps we left him, it was never completely clear. Good at languages, always wanted to travel. Childhood ambitions ranged from astronaut to private eye to diplomat. Followed in absent father's footsteps for a while (don't ask me why) and studied law at a regional university. Hated it. Didn't finish. Took a gap year, added a second one, and travelled (Middle East, Africa, the Americas). Returned with the intention of joining the Foreign Service, procrastinated, and then buggered about for way too long in various odd jobs before finally settling on the SIS and successfully applying for my current job of intelligence officer. And excepting the odd love affair, that, sad to say, was my relatively uneventful life in a nutshell.

And yes, so there I was, your bog standard, lost-in-the-background British intelligence agent abroad, stretched out in the sun with his sunglasses and his book. And doing what he was paid to do: thinking.

Dala was now going by the name of Chantal Fabre. I'd discovered this in Paris, between Dala's departure and my own, so at least I'd managed to use the twenty-four hours constructively. Same appearance, according to the fake passport she was using, so presumably she'd ditched the red wig before she boarded her flight. In other words it was back to the dark-blonde look that was so firmly implanted in my head. While a person's looks were obviously an indispensable piece of information for someone in my position, in Dala's case her physical attractiveness was an unfortunate, unerasable distraction.

I wondered if she knew she was being followed. She had to assume that an effort was being made to track her down, but call it instinct (which, after Geneva, I'd never overrule again), something told me she wasn't aware of any specific person following her. I doubted, in other words, that she was aware of *me*. So she wasn't really toying with me, she was just doing those things that people like her do: leave false trails, evade the world.

My thoughts were interrupted by a small crowd of resorters who appeared to have materialised out of thin air, but had probably escaped from one of the conference centres. The men of the contingent were removing their shirts with unjustified glee and generally lounging about in their boardshorts. One of them launched himself into the pool with a tsunami of a splash and attempted to do laps, slaloming around a pod of shrieking children. The women were all in swimming costumes too, either one-pieces or bikinis, quite modest on the whole – at least by Western standards – although I couldn't help but notice one girl, apparently called Kat, in a skimpy pink crochet bikini veiled like an afterthought by a see-through gauze resort shirt, and another in a micro-G-string that was really more of an accessory. There was an eruption of laughter as someone made fun of someone else.

I couldn't picture Dala as one of them, somehow.

They collectively turned up the volume, and I later learned my tranquillity had just been invaded by a conference of Australian accountants. Something made me think of volcanoes, possibly my recent experience with the ash cloud, and realising that Indonesia – constituting one branch of the Ring of Fire – was just across the water, I imagined the accountants being dropped, one by one, into a bright red, bubbling lake of lava.

And after this virtual massacre was over, my thoughts returned to Dala. As they increasingly did, these days. Understandable, really, given she'd become my sole project. But I realise now that in incremental steps I was gradually becoming more and more preoccupied, not so much with her, but with the *idea* of her.

4.

SHE THEN disappeared like a puff of steam.

Somehow I lost the trail completely and didn't pick it up again for almost two months. My patience and hard work, however, were ultimately rewarded because this time I managed to catch up with more than a mere lingering sense of her, more than just a name in a ledger. This time I found her in person. At a hotel in Bangkok.

For the life of me though, I can no longer remember the name of the place. The Majestic?

No longer holding herself out as Chantal Fabre, now she was using an Italian passport and going by the name of Paola Leonetti. As soon as I traced her, I thought OK, I can work with that. Paola. Paola Leonetti. *Paola*. I practised saying her name. Practised what my story would be, my opening gambit. And as I did so, it occurred to me: I was planning to speak with her. Before reporting her location to Alan. I tried not to think of the implications of that.

I didn't know where this plan came from, this plan to talk to her. I only knew that I had to. It wasn't even a question. It should have been, but it wasn't. Not at that point, anyway.

Once I'd found the hotel she was staying in, I went straight there, wasted no time. Not after two months! I think I almost ran there, through those colourful, crowded streets.

And finally seeing her again – and meeting her – it happened in such a way that the whole thing, now, feels more like a fantasy than a memory.

The hotel was on a busy road and had a rundown, anarchic feel to it. Definitely one for the backpackers. Its facade was covered in soft-drink advertising, but what I remember in particular was that at street level, next to the front entrance, there was a barber shop. This I can recall with the utmost clarity not just because I went in there for a shave as soon as I arrived – don't ask me why, it was an odd thing to do, I know – but because at the precise moment the barber pulled out his cut-throat razor and struck the pose, ready to begin, I caught a glimpse of her through the shop window.

Dala.

Or should I say Paola. Minus the red wig, and blonde-haired again, she was walking past wearing a green t-shirt and emphatically frayed, cut-away denim shorts faded almost to white.

I have to be honest, I was powerless to do anything but stare.

And for a split second, her gaze met mine, through that window. Nothing registered though and there was no locking of eyes, confirming my assumption that to her I was still just another person in another city. She simply turned away and strode on into the hotel as if she owned it.

And the barber got on with his job.

She was, I guessed, posing as a backpacker, this woman of many names. And as I sat there, I wondered who the real woman was, underneath the clothes and the olive skin.

Δ

No-one could be sure, but our best guess was that Dala had grown up in Paris, the daughter of a French father and a Russian mother. Siblings unclear, but she was believed to have had a half-sister via the mother and a half-brother via the father. If we were right, her father was Paul Gasnier, an overbearing bully who was abusive towards his wife. Paul Gasnier was a businessman who suddenly disappeared one day. His wife, Elena, claimed he'd run off with another woman, but the word on the street was that Elena's Russian connections had been involved, and that he'd been killed.

I imagined that someone in Dala's position would grow up with a fascination for stories.

Δ

Half an hour later, at the conclusion of my barbershop experience, I entered the hotel.

Just to the left of a small reception desk, manned by a

middle-aged male transfixed by a miniature TV, was what can only best be described as a vestibule ('lobby' would be overstating it). The room was modestly proportioned, with a large, shuttered window to the street admitting light, and decorated with attempts at retro cool. Old racing car stickers, a framed *Thunderbirds Are Go* poster, a Malibu surfboard stretching the length of the far wall. And Dala.

She was standing next to a lava lamp, and chatting to two young men: American backpackers Stephan and Fred, travelling buddies from Charlotte, North Carolina. As luck would have it, I'd already met them – it's a habit of mine to speak to everybody, for precisely this kind of pay-off – and one of them acknowledged me, saying 'Hey, buddy!' and giving me the in that I wanted.

I wandered over. It wasn't far, it was a small room.

'How's it going?' I addressed my question to Stephan, the more outgoing of the two Americans.

'Yeah, great. This is, er… Paola.'

'John,' I said quickly, saving Stephan the embarrassment.

Dala didn't offer her hand, just nodded and smiled at me. 'Hi.'

So natural, so innocent.

'Paola's from Florence, right?' Stephan said. '*Firenze*, sorry. *Firenze*.'

'*Si*, very close,' she said. 'Not so far.' Her voice was soft and mellifluous, yet strong. Conveyed that adorable and typically Italian sense of a suppressed shout.

When Stephan started talking about a themed bar he and

Fred had discovered down the road, I got a chance to examine Dala's face at close quarters. The perfect skin, the gleaming, blue-green eyes. Her dark blonde hair, pulled back in a youthful ponytail this time, seemed an even deeper shade than before. But it suited her, and she made a good backpacker. A good Italian too, for that matter – not just in her voice, she had just the right bright vivacity about her overall demeanour. Of course, it was possible I was imagining the Italian-ness, but if I was, that was surely part of the trick. It's certainly a talent, being someone you're not, I thought to myself, admiring her.

I imagined I could detect, too, the faintest of smirks on her face. She wasn't looking at me, almost making a point of *not* looking at me. It was as if she could sense my admiration and, dare I say it, was enjoying it.

A plan was drawn up – a plan to meet up for a drink at the themed bar, the four of us, Stephan, Fred, John and Paola – and all the while, in the lava lamp that remained in my sightline over Dala's left shoulder, red magma-like blobs soundlessly crashed into each other in slow motion.

Δ

Before the four of us met up again, I had time to think, properly think about what I was doing. I think I knew I should have been calling Alan at that point, giving him a heads-up. There was an agreed meeting place, I'd soon be in a position to maintain a visual, and it would have been the perfect time to call in backup – presumably a branch of the

Thai intelligence service – and have her placed into custody and shipped off to wherever (not for me to ask).

But I didn't make the call.

Why didn't I? I'd done my job and done it well: given the slipperiness of the target, I'd be able to expect a big pat on the back and feel I'd more than made up for my previous failures. What's more, I knew if I didn't call I'd be heading into dangerous territory and arguably acting beyond the scope of my instructions.

So why didn't I make that call? I told myself that I needed to establish a greater degree of certainty, that she might have sensed something and never show up later as planned. But deep down I knew this wasn't the reason. Call it curiosity, call it lust, or call it the ongoing problem I've always had with authority, but the real reason, I suspect, was that she'd already, even at this early stage, cast a spell over me. A spell cast not just by Dala herself, but also, as I've already mentioned, by the idea of her, that cunning little virus that had now been growing in my head for two months. Meeting her just made the problem a whole lot worse.

And just like a person succumbing to an illness, I simply wasn't thinking straight.

Δ

Like the hotel, I can no longer recall the name of the bar, or its theme – it was maybe cowboys or robots or both – but the level of alcohol consumption made the night a little hazy. And I had my mind on other things.

I remember her showing me a fake Chanel keyring she'd bought that day – fake diamonds set in fake silver, in the shape of Chanel's overlapping double C logo. She laughed about it, saying she loved fake things, that they made such a statement. *In Italy,* she said, *we revel in imitation. All fashion is fraud and is all the more beautiful for that. And Bangkok is the king of counterfeit.*

I can't remember what else we all talked about. And I can't tell you at what point everything changed. But everything did. What I remember is suddenly realising that Dala had stopped avoiding my eyes. She'd begun to flirt with me. What started as an almost accidental crossing of gazes, became a lingering expression of desire.

I was, literally, powerless to resist. It wasn't my fault.

Many, many drinks later, with Stephan and Fred passing swiftly into their tabernacle of anaesthetised drunkenness, and Dala and I sunken together in our own private banquette of delight, the suggestion was made, by Dala, that she and I return to the hotel, and leave our friends to continue on their own cowboy-merry way.

Her arm was pushing vitally against mine, our hands touching. One of us said something silly. The other one laughed. Our faces were close. Hers was a silhouette, but the whites of her eyes shone in the pulsing gloom. In perfect synchronicity, we leaned in at the same time, our lips connecting in what felt like a crash of interstellar proportions.

And then it was back to the hotel, past reception and the modest vestibule with its surfboard wall, and up the creaky wooden stairs to the rooms above. Conforming to a tacit agreement – there was no discussion about it – we went to my room, room 15 (for some reason I remember that and not the name of the hotel), all wood-panelled walls and floorboards like the rest of the hotel, and bare like my empty soul. Except it wasn't empty that night, it was full of the celebration of female beauty.

The creaking stairs and floorboards, then, led us to the squeaking old-fashioned bed on which we collapsed in an eruption of furious, mind-blowing lust. And afterwards, my mind indeed felt blown: ruptured, like a torrent of molten rock bursting from a vent.

Which is possibly why I've forgotten the name of the hotel. The Regal? The Royale? Something to do with royalty, anyway. Something fit for a queen, you might say. Not that I was putting her on a pedestal. Not quite then, at any rate.

I don't think.

Δ

There was one conversation I do remember. We were on the bed. It was late (or early). I was saying something and it slipped out. Too many drinks. I called her Dala.

'What?' she said. Her facial expression changed. Or maybe I imagined it did, maybe it was too dark to see her face.

'Hmm?' I knew immediately what I'd done. Knew it as those two beautiful syllables were sliding past my lips.

'What did you call me?'

'Paola.' I made it sound as close to Dala as I could: *Parla*.

It was fortunate they sounded so similar, Dala and Paola, especially in my drawling slur of an accent. She seemed to buy it.

'Lucky for you,' she said, smiling I think. 'I thought it might have been your ex-girlfriend's name. In which case you would now be dead.'

5.

Saturday, 19 June
Hotel __?, Bangkok, Thailand

SHE WAS like a spirit, or a dream.

Or a beautiful thought.

I hadn't realised I'd fallen asleep, not deeply asleep, but I must have, because when I opened my eyes the sun was up and Dala was gone.

There was no sign she'd even been there, except for one thing: in her hurry, she'd forgotten her fake Chanel keyring. It must have fallen out of her bag. It was lying next to the bed, where her bag had been, and now it was the only proof that I hadn't imagined the whole thing.

Naturally I tried to find her, knocked on the door of her room, asked the new face at reception, but I already knew the answer. She'd checked out.

What did I expect? I know what I wanted: I wanted the normal rules not to apply, I wanted something completely out of the ordinary to happen – I wanted her to have fallen for me so quickly that she'd throw caution to the wind – put her life and liberty at risk – and stay with me. As much as I wanted this, though, I knew as well as anyone else that the fall of the cards is almost always dictated by the way they're stacked. And thus, she'd gone.

Which left me in a quandary. What was I to do?

Strictly in terms of my job, my duty was to get out there immediately, chase down every lead and find her again. Then phone it in, close the case. But things had suddenly become more complicated. In not reporting her location at the hotel, not to mention our little 'indiscretion', I'd crossed a line. I now had a serious conflict of interest on my hands. Even if I was to somehow ignore the indiscretion, there was no way I could now disclose finding her without exposing myself to all manner of awkward questions. I'd have to keep the whole episode quiet – turn it into a 'false history' and bury it. So I was already compromised to an extent, assuming I carried on with my duties. Not to mention 'the deal'. With Alan.

No more mistakes. This failure to report must never happen again, OK? Ever. That's the deal.

Or I could quit. It would be better for my sanity. And it wasn't as if I desperately needed the money. I had access to a respectable sum tucked away in a savings account and earning interest, a little nest egg I'd built up over the years (I hadn't, after all, ever had anything much to spend it on). Or, if not quit, I could at least telephone Alan, tell him I'd reached a dead end, and ask to be put on another case. Tell him a fresh pair of eyes may be all that was required.

The trouble was, this job, this case, was the one thing that connected me to Dala. Not that I told myself that at the time. I simply decided I had to soldier on. Pretend to myself, and to my superiors if it ever came to it, that it never occurred to me – not in my wildest dreams – that Paola Leonetti and Dala Gasnier were the same person. What I was going to do when I next found her I didn't know, but soldiering on was a way of keeping my options open.

This decision to continue was not a quick one and I agonised over it for most of the morning. I needn't have bothered. Because just after I'd made up my mind, Alan called.

When I saw the number come up on my phone, I panicked. Almost didn't answer it. I knew, though, that false histories needed to be buried today, not tomorrow. Especially the true ones.

'Any luck?' was all he said. No greeting. Bad sign.

'Mixed.'

'You getting close?'

'Realistically, weeks rather than days.'

'Return for a meeting. Post-haste.'

And then he ended the call.

6.

SHE TOOK possession of my fitful dreams on that flight back to London.

My waking hours, though, were plagued by worry: most of it born of repeated analysis of that last phone call – ad nauseam – and a deep, stifling fear over why I was being recalled and what Alan had in store for me.

It couldn't come fast enough, the cab to Vauxhall, the arrival at that belligerent edifice on the banks of the Thames, the view of the forging river through tinted glass from a hard chair at a large table in a vast empty room. And then at last, the end of the endless waiting (because I *knew* he'd make a point of keeping me waiting) signalled by the arrival of Alan himself.

He greeted but didn't look at me as he entered the room, and I tried to analyse his movements, but he gave nothing away. And when he did look at me – the pale blue eyes, the round face – the sensation of being judged gave rise to a pain that was almost physical. He was an old hand: that cold stare was a lethal weapon and I felt sure he could read me like an x-ray, but I did my level best to radiate calm fortitude – I worked hard at channelling the building we were sitting in.

He seemed to relax a little. Asked me about my flight, and the food in Bangkok, and complained about the June weather in London, the so-called summer. It's the summer solstice tomorrow, you realise, he said. Ah yes, I replied.

And then he paused. Here it comes, I thought.

'I was thinking you might want to take your annual leave early this year,' he said. 'In the meantime, with respect to SANDPIPER, you could pass the baton, as it were, to someone else. We could move you to another op when you got back. I can assure you it would be no less... interesting.'

He waited for me to respond. I didn't know how to. *Does he know?* was all I could think.

'Oh?' I said, rather lamely.

'You can get caught in a rut with cases like these. And anyway, the Service is well-served by moving its officers around. Broadening experiences.'

He waited again.

'I don't know what to say.'

'I understand,' he said. 'The fact of the matter is, this is something I always do with this type of operation. I know what it can do to a man's, or a person's head. I always call them back, and encourage early leave, but I never insist. It remains the officer's decision.'

'I see.'

'It's no reflection on you or your work.'

I nodded, thoughtfully on the outside. Inside, massively relieved. *He doesn't know.*

I should have said yes. I should have taken up his offer. I would have been saved.

'Take some time to think about it,' Alan said. 'Sleep on it.'

'Thank you, but if it's all right with you, I'd just as soon carry on.'

'It's your decision.'

'I'm enjoying it, to be honest. I think I'm making progress.'

Alan didn't look convinced. He looked, dare I say it, troubled. And for a man renowned for his poker face, that was an achievement.

'As I say, it's your decision,' he said. 'And if you're enjoying it, that's the main thing. It's a good sign. Promising.'

He stared at me for a moment, hard. My toes clenched.

'Off you go then,' he said finally. 'Go get 'em.'

'Thanks. I appreciate it.'

'Don't forget our deal. Everything. To me.'

'Everything,' I said to him, nodding.

And then I was gone.

7.

Tuesday, 12 October
Nouméa, New Caledonia

'SHE'S IN New Caledonia.'

It was my number one South Pacific asset. Fijian. With him, though, I never knew if it was the truth – a red hot tip – or simply the kava talking.

'In Nouméa,' he added.

'How do you know?'

'Let's just say a friend of a friend of a friend told me.'

'Sounds like a super-spreader. Or common knowledge at best. Should I be paying for that?'

'Common knowledge is the truest knowledge. And the true stuff is what you pay me for, right boss?'

And I couldn't argue with that.

Δ

I was standing on a footpath in central Nouméa, looking through an old wrought iron fence at a stately, two-storey colonial building with deep verandas. The tropical sun was beating down hard out of a clear, unforgiving sky. The building, girdled by dark green trees and deep shade, emanated a cool peace, but there was something else: an air of mystery perhaps, or a mood that told me that something was about to happen. I suppose you'd call it a high-octane hunch.

Δ

It had been over three months, and I'd been getting desperate. Returning to Bangkok from London had resulted in too many nights spent in too many bars, drinking way too many Singha beers and Sicilian Bastards. Not once did I consider changing my mind and taking up Alan's offer. I was a man on a mission, in every sense. This singular determination was epitomized, in a way, by the fake Chanel keyring – I found it in the bottom of my suitcase one day. I wondered why I still had it with me. I was hardly intending to return it to her. It was no use to me, it wasn't going to help me catch her, it was just extra weight. I won't say I was treasuring it, exactly. Maybe it was a kind of nostalgia, although I didn't think I was the sentimental type.

And maybe, like Dala, I liked fake things too?

I was certainly *becoming* more of one. Because like Dala, I'd adopted a new nationality: I was now officially Canadian, courtesy of Alan. With a new name too. Just for this part of the operation, just for Asia. Not my idea, but Alan seemed to think I'd benefit from a temporary 'change of persona'. I wasn't sure if the Canadians were in on this, but I knew not to ask.

Anyway, there'd been hopeful leads, and even a few near misses. And I'd obediently reported them all back to Alan, everything, as per our deal. After all, I had to keep myself in the game and avoid being called back again. But the disappointments were piling up, the trail had gone cold, and Asia, as Alan had said, was a big place.

And then I'd remembered something Dala had said to me on that lust-infused night in the nameless hotel. (Fragments were still coming back to me, as if they'd been pages of a book, torn-out and haphazardly returned by a capricious wind.)

Δ

We were naked, she was on her stomach and I was straddling her, knees tucked against her hips, and pressing the heels of my hands into her tanned back and upwards along the beautiful undulation of her spine.

'Where would you be, if you could be anywhere, right now?' I asked her.

'Here is just fine.'

'But where else? Right now.'

'Somewhere in the South Pacific. On a tropical beach, with white sand and coconut palms. With you doing *that*.'

'White sand and coconut palms, that is so clichéd, Dala.'

'What?' She'd raised and turned her head, so I could see her face in profile.

'Hmm?'

'What did you call me?'

Δ

The South Pacific. It had been worth a shot so I'd focussed my efforts there, eventually receiving the New Caledonia tip-off from my kava enthusiast.

New Caledonia though, it didn't quite make sense. It was a French territory, so even though the language would have made it easier for blending in, it would also have made arresting her a far simpler exercise. (Which suggested my informant may have been exaggerating when he described her presence in Nouméa as being 'common knowledge'.) Perhaps she had a crazy streak – an idea, I had to admit, that I found appealing – or perhaps going somewhere that made no sense was a part of her modus operandi, a way of staying a step ahead. Or it was both, more likely.

So I'd flown to Nouméa and spent two days walking the streets. I kept thinking I was seeing her, of course, in every tourist shop, and every marketplace. Looking back, I'm sure I really did see her, at least once. I'd see her though, and she'd disappear again, like a ghost.

Seeing the colourful fish laid out on ice in the Fish Market, made me think of what would become of her once they had her. After I betrayed her location.

('Betrayed' rather than 'reported', note. Because, already,

the way I thought about her had changed. *I* had changed.)

I'd then been informed, via a third party, of a possible sighting: at the airport two weeks earlier, a customs officer with a liking for cash had witnessed his colleague stamp the passport of an arriving passenger who loosely fitted Dala's description. The customs officer and his colleague had both taken a shine to her. And so if it was indeed Dala – and I, for one, was certain that it was – then she was now Jasmine Carroll, French citizen, English by birth, and here on holiday. Here, no doubt, to spend time on white, sandy beaches fringed with coconut palms.

By this stage I'd spent so much time thinking about her, it had been easy to put myself in her shoes. So easy that the resulting scenario, rather than simply being the work of a fertile imagination, could almost have been a memory.

It's an unexpected relief, arriving in French-speaking New Caledonia. It strikes her as she passes through customs control at the airport. While her English is excellent, and she's even begun to forget the occasional word in French, it's a comfort all the same to be back among French speakers. Which is a little surprising, given that she's always felt like a foreigner, even growing up in France, and regarded that feeling as being her natural state.

You'd think the customs officers at Tontouta International airport would be used to all types, but the man who stamps her passport seems to have trouble knowing what to make of this Jasmine Carroll, a Parisian of English birth, radiating more confidence than a film star. Not knowing what to make of her, though, doesn't stop him from wanting her, she can see that in his eyes. If there's one thing she can always do well, it's make an entrance.

This thought makes her smile as, an hour or so later, she walks down the Place des Cocotiers in the town's centre. Nouméa is her sort of town, too. Small, but surprisingly anonymous; a girl like me, she thinks, I could be happy here. As if to confirm the thought, a local teenager sharing hip hop dance moves with his circle of friends flashes his smiling white teeth at her as she passes by under the coconut palms.

Why does she crave invisibility so much? Obviously there's the series of events that led to her departure from France, but it goes further back than that, back to even before she began writing as a journalist under a pen name. Whatever the cause, it's an immutable part of her, one of the few things that never changes.

And being one of her few unchanging qualities, it is this deep-seated tendency to disguise herself, and to hide from the rest of the world, that paradoxically both casts her adrift on the ocean of uncertainty that her life has become, and at the same time helps to anchor her, with its comforting familiarity, and thus to find herself.

Δ

All of which led me to this particular footpath in the centre of town, just around the corner from my hotel. The building I was standing outside of, in that hot midday sun, a relic of the colonial era (which for New Caledonia had not entirely disappeared), was, according to a plaque on the footpath, the Bernheim Library. It had been built in Paris for the 1900 Exposition – it was the New Caledonia pavilion – and had been dismantled and rebuilt in Nouméa in 1902. And as I stood there, feeling that something was about to happen, I experienced an even stranger sensation: I knew – not just thought, but knew – that Dala was inside.

What better place, perhaps, for a fugitive seeking refuge from the sun and the world around them? Refuge from all that is the present?

Inside, bamboo ceiling fans whirl through the silent air and below, books that reek of the past line the camphorated shelves. As she strolls inside, relishing the library's quiet anonymity, she takes a moment to marvel at the kind of mind it takes to dream up edifices such as these. What kind of perfection were they attempting to imitate?

What kind of perfection, for that matter, is she *trying to imitate in this endless quest of hers? What is she striving for?*

Solo locals with daypacks dotted the grounds, heading into and out of the building in quiet pensiveness. I made my way up the shaded pathway, through a quadrangle and entered the library beneath a gabled portico. Through the front door and stepped inside, into the main room. Took in the vista: tropical light pouring in through large, latticed windows onto a bright, white floor; hardwood staircase and balustrades; bare desks populated with silent readers; rows and stacks of books.

I didn't see her straight away.

I must have walked right past her, because when I reached the end of the room and turned to look back towards the main entrance, there she was. Brown hair this time rather than the more familiar dark blonde, but she was wearing the same green t-shirt and frayed denim shorts as she'd been wearing in Bangkok, and she was almost looking straight at me, so I recognized her immediately. Those beautiful blue eyes again (or were they green?). I'm surprised she didn't see me, but she was in the process of getting up from a desk and heading for the front door.

I had to fight the almost overwhelming instinct to greet her. Alan, though, was in my head. Not only was this what I'd sacrificed almost six months of my life for, but it was likely to be the last chance I'd get to fix the mess I'd made of things. The last chance to save my job. The last chance to save *myself.*

And so I followed her at a safe distance, but first made a detour via the desk she'd been sitting at. She'd left a book open: it was a large-format hardback with an old-fashioned design – *Volcanoes Of The Earth* by Fred M. Bullard – and on the front cover was a large photographic image of an erupting volcano. All I could think about was the ash cloud debacle.

But the wave of depression was only fleeting, I had a job to do. I hurried out into the bright sunshine.

She was walking quickly along the hot footpaths, past cafes and clothes shops, and I had to hurry to stay in sight of her. She reached a bus stop, and almost magically a bus appeared. I didn't think I could avoid being spotted, so didn't follow her on. Didn't know quite what I could do other than take a note of the bus number, but a rare taxi appeared – a minor miracle – and I grabbed it.

'Suivez ce bus,' I said to the driver. *Follow that bus.*

And so we did. Past the luxury yachts at Port Moselle and the frolickers at Baie des Citrons, and on past the overwater restaurant at Anse Vata. At each bus stop we pulled over, keeping our distance, and I scrutinized the alighting passengers. I'm not sure what the taxi driver thought I was doing, but it couldn't have been anything good. Eventually, at a bus stop near the southern end of the Nouméa peninsula, I spotted her getting off. I generously tipped the driver and followed on foot.

I followed her along a path through some trees and down to Le Méridien, another tropical resort nestled in lush greenery. These resorts, they seemed to be her thing – although I couldn't see how they'd help with flying under the radar.

Negotiating a circular driveway and fountain, I strolled in through the front entrance and into the cool of the reception area with its white-tiled floor and dark, hardwood furniture. I was wearing a cap with the visor pulled down low, so felt anonymous enough to remove my sunglasses. I was just in time to catch a glimpse of Dala heading to the lifts.

In this era of magnetic keycards, gone are the days when you could watch someone collecting their key at reception and note their room number. I couldn't risk getting into the lift with her, but decided the task would be more easily executed another way. I spoke to one of the receptionists, a haughty brunette: she was young, white and French, most likely spending a year or two in the welcoming warmth of the South Pacific before heading back to the colder and more familial comforts of home.

'I'd like to leave a message for a Miss Jasmine Carroll. She's in room...' I trailed off, as if trying to remember.

'Let me check, sir.' She typed something and stared at her screen. 'Yes, sir, she's in Room 509. What message would you like to leave?'

'Actually it's all right, there's something I need to check first.'

I made my way over to a herd of beige sofas and sat down on one of them, pretending to look at my phone. I wasn't looking though, I was thinking.

It was time. I had the country, the city, the hotel name, the room number, and a confirmed visual only seconds old. There would never be a better moment to call Alan. It would make up for all my mistakes and omissions – all would be forgiven. What's more, it would be a huge feather in my cap. Promotion. Celebration.

And yet, I did nothing.

It wasn't even a case of getting cold feet, or not exactly. The moment I sat down on that sofa, I realised that since seeing her in the library – and possibly all along – I never had any intention of making the call. Not at that point at least. There was something else I had to do first.

What I didn't realise, was that I was already caught in a web. A web largely of my own making.

Δ

And so I decided to leave a message after all.

I almost returned to face the haughty receptionist again, but I wanted to remain as inconspicuous as possible, and I also wanted to be well clear of the place before the message was delivered. So I walked out the door and retreated to my hotel in the centre of town, the Hôtel Le Paris, and then gave it another hour just to be safe. I was pleased when a male receptionist answered my call.

8.

Wednesday, 13 October
Nouméa, New Caledonia

SHE REREADS the note for the umpteenth time.

> Dear Jasmine. Know about alpine lake. Fish in net
> but prefer to throw back. Have proposition. Beach
> restaurant, 11am tomorrow, Wednesday.
> Duologue. All cards on table. Nothing to lose and
> everything to gain. Love J.

She doesn't experience the rising panic that she felt when she first read it after finding it slipped under the door of her room the previous afternoon – she'd almost checked out then and there, before calming herself down and seeing sense – but the light of the new day hasn't altogether removed a lingering sense of unease, either. Still, whoever this 'J' is, she guesses he or she is probably right about one thing: she doesn't have anything to lose.

And anyway, their objective couldn't be to pull her in, otherwise they'd have already done it. They clearly think they have a proposition that would appeal to her. And who knows, maybe it would? Being on the run, even in a tropical paradise, has its limitations.

Or at least, that's how I was hoping she would have taken it. Something along those lines. It was certainly what I was banking on.

Why did I leave a message like that? Why did I decide to put my cards on the table straight away? I knew it was a risk. But my assessment was that she wouldn't run, not until she'd first heard my proposal. Otherwise I'd be a one-night stand come back to haunt her, suddenly exposed as the enemy. Without a pre-laid hint of there being a deal to be made, it'd only be confrontational. And potentially ugly. I may not have been in this game very long, but I knew enough to know that operatives like her were capable of almost anything. You didn't want to scare them. It was going to be confronting enough when she discovered who I was, but at least she'd already know I had a proposition for her, and that I wasn't about to call the cops.

Another reason was that it committed me to a course of action. There'd be no more hesitation, only a forward movement towards who knew what.

And what's all this about a proposition? I hear you ask. Where did that come from? Especially when I was supposed to be doing my job and calling in her location to Alan.

Clearly that virus in my brain had been hard at work, putting together this little package.

Δ

10.55am. The outdoor restaurant at Le Méridien was still filling up as the lazier resort guests – the lovers, the alcoholics, the miscellaneous unbreakfasted – began to turn the trickle into a flood. The heat, too, had arrived, and along with it, the glare. Sunglasses were an essential accessory, although it wasn't just for the brightness that I was wearing mine.

The restaurant was located where the grounds of the resort ended and the beach began. Beyond the narrow strip of sand, dotted with clusters of sunbathers, it was blue water and bright sky all the way to the ocean's perfect horizon. The occasional kitesurfer slid past, taking advantage of an early, stiff breeze. Of course, Le Méridien was a tropical resort like all the others: there were trees, and there was water. And the sounds of three kinds of splashing, from the fountains, the pools, and the ocean. There was the constant struggle for supremacy between a sense of tranquillity – championed by the breeze through the leaves of the palm trees – and a sense of gaiety. And here, in the outdoor restaurant with its insistent hubbub, it was gaiety that clearly had the upper hand.

As I snaked my way between the peopled tables, I scanned the multicultural faces. And to my great relief, hers was one of them.

She was easy to spot. At a table on her own, in the far

corner of the restaurant area. Short white dress, mahogany-brown hair pulled into a ponytail. Beach hat and sunglasses, tanned olive skin casually greeting the sun. She was 'holiday' personified.

She already had a coffee in front of her, which told me she'd turned up early, so she was treating this seriously, but at the same time was relaxed about it. In control. Her head was angled slightly away from me, but I wasn't fooled – I knew she would have already spotted me and, as I altered course to head in her direction, would have been watching me behind her sunglasses with those striking eyes of hers.

By the time I'd arrived at her table, she'd turned to face me. She left her sunglasses on and so did I, preserving a degree of mutual anonymity. There was no immediate sign of recognition, which didn't surprise me, and not just because I was wearing sunglasses. It had, after all, been one drunken night, almost four months ago. And who knew how many of those she'd had since.

Also, right now, she would have been expecting another type of person altogether, a new face, not some guy she'd slept with in Bangkok.

'Excuse me,' I said. 'I believe you may have dropped this?'

I held out my hand and showed her the fake Chanel keyring.

At first she gave it only the most perfunctory of glances, before looking back at me – no doubt assuming it was simply an attempt at one of those typically bland greetings frequently adopted by undercover agents meeting in public. I may as well have said *didn't we meet in Bucharest last summer?*

'I don't think so,' she said. 'It must be someone else's.' She spoke good English with just the faintest of French accents – Paola Leonetti was a distant memory. She was good, this one.

'Are you sure?' I persisted.

She smiled again and then humoured me by turning her attention back to the keyring.

'Yes, I'm quite sure. It's not mine.' She was about to turn away but did a double-take and furrowed her brow. 'At least, I don't think...' She raised her sunglasses for a closer inspection. Lowered them again, and looked up, examining me for a moment. Was it coming back to her? Needless to say, the penny, if it hadn't quite dropped yet, was through the slot and in freefall.

'Where did you find it?'

'Just over there.' I pointed.

'On the beach? Ah. Well then, no, I haven't been—'

'In Bangkok.'

She froze for a few seconds, and stared at me. And then she reanimated, and visibly relaxed. Frowned, and smiled at the same time.

'Oh my god.'

'Paola, right?'

She nodded mutely, clearly trying to remember my name, and possibly also toying with the idea of reviving her Italian accent.

'Been a while,' I said and smiled. Removed my sunglasses.

'It's so great to see you,' she said, with apparent enthusiasm.

She removed her own sunglasses, to get a better look at me. And there they were again, her extraordinary eyes. Eyes the colour of the iridescent sea beyond the palms. And they were smiling too. Was she actually pleased to see me? Not for long.

'Jeff,' I said. 'Jeff Perry.'

'Jeff,' she repeated, the name obviously ringing no bells. 'Yes. Of course.'

A serious look, uncertainty creeping back in. She was no longer relaxed.

'Mind if I join you?'

'I… Sure. I'm expecting someone in a few minutes, though.' She looked over my shoulder. 'This is… How are you? What are you doing here?'

'Same as you I expect. Holiday. Yeah?'

'Yeah. And so… wow. You've been carrying that keyring all this time?'

'Been using it actually. Ever since you left it in my room. In that hotel, whatever its name was.'

'John,' she said abruptly. 'You told me your name was—'

'It's Jeff.'

She just looked at me. Here we go, I thought.

'And maybe we should keep things on a strictly *false-name* basis. Don't you think… Jasmine?'

'Huh,' was all she said, accompanied by another frown. She leant back in her chair, sizing me up and assessing this new information.

I took a deep breath and added:

'Or perhaps you'd prefer *Dala*.'

A flicker of fear flashed across her eyes and she looked around again, checking for signs of an ambush.

'Don't worry,' I said. 'Your secret's safe with me, as they say.'

'Who are you?'

'I told you.' Just for the hell of it, I tweaked my accent, introduced a hint of Canadian: 'I'm Jeff Perry, Canadian, born in Vancouver. That's to say, I'm Jeff Perry no less than you're Jasmine Carroll, French and born in London.' Then returned to my usual accent: 'Or... no less than you're Dala Gasnier, I'm John Penne and British.'

'And?' she said, with a hint of irritation. 'I suppose you wrote that note.'

'I did.'

'So you're... Who do you work for?'

'I need to explain something first.'

'Just tell me who.' She was cross, now, you could tell. Was she shaking?

'I'll tell you,' I said. 'But you need to hear me out.'

'You've been following me. Since... Before Bangkok.'

'Yes. Since Geneva.'

'Since Geneva,' she repeated.

'You gave me the slip at the train station. With a little help from a red wig.'

Forgive me if I don't smile, her eyes seemed to be saying. I continued:

'And then you gave me the slip at Charles de Gaulle, with a little help from an ash cloud. From Eyja... whatever its name is.'

'Eyjafjallajökull,' she said, nailing the name of that Icelandic culprit without missing a beat. (And now I've mastered it too: *ay-yah fyat-la yer-kuhtl*.)

'That's the one. But listen, I—'

'You're a British agent.'

'No.'

Technically not, at least. I was a British intelligence officer. Not an agent who got his hands dirty. Although I had to admit, for an intelligence officer, my hands were beginning to look distinctly grubby these days.

'Kind of,' I added.

'Kind of.'

'I have been acting for the British, yes, but everything's in a state of flux. You really need to hear me out, here. This is where the proposition—'

'So you were *acting* for the British, were you, when you slept with me in Bangkok? Pretending to be John...'

She'd already forgotten my surname again. You could hardly blame her, I suppose.

'Penne. I *am* John Penne.'

'Pretending to be John Penne the English tourist,' she said, seething, 'not John Penne *the British agent*!' Despite her emphatic delivery, she was managing to keep her voice down.

'I'm not a British agent, not—'

'Whatever! What you did, it was…' She was searching for the words. One word, as it turned out, which she spat at me. 'It was *rape*.'

She was still keeping it down, but she remained clearly livid. A pale, red-haired kid at the next table was staring, and his parents were shooting us glances, *not in our paradise please, take your nasty domestics elsewhere if you don't mind…*

'I don't think it was quite—'

'Of course it was, you can't do that. You can't just sleep with someone on… on… on *false pretences*.'

'It wasn't a pretence. It wasn't false, it was genuine. What about you, with your Paola Leonetti charade. An Italian backpacker, how was that not false? At least I was John Penne. And *then* you disappeared on me.'

'Poor you, poor baby.'

'Listen. I had nothing to gain, sleeping with you. Not in terms of my career anyway. I had nothing to gain and everything to lose. My job was to report your location. Which I *didn't do*. Think about that for a moment.'

This seemed to settle her down. She made a little conciliatory noise, a begrudging kind of grunt. I stared back at the neighbouring family to encourage them to mind their own business.

When I turned back, she was looking away herself, out to the horizon. I waited patiently as she watched a kitesurfer skitter by.

'So you have a proposition for me,' she said eventually.

'I do. First though, there's one thing I don't get. In the

Alps, the body in the lake. She was one of ours, obviously, and we know, the whole *world* knows that you were responsible.'

No reaction. So I forged on.

'Why would you do that? And even if it was an accident, which is one of the theories circulating, what were you trying to do? You *were with* them, weren't you? The French, I mean. So this woman, she was on your side. She was one of ours. So she was on your side too. Wasn't she? It simply makes no sense, unless…'

I let that hang. Still nothing. I continued:

'They've been co-operating, incidentally. Your people. The French. About time.' I paused. 'They're calling you a *rogue agent*, you know, so… I have to assume that's what you are.'

'Would that bother you?' she asked. Finally, a reaction.

'No. There but for the grace of God, and all that. In fact, maybe now, maybe I'm one myself. So no, it wouldn't worry me. Depending on who you're *now* acting for, of course.'

Silence. I waited. Somewhere an outboard motor roared into life. The seconds ticked by. Felt like hours, but I held my nerve.

'I have a funny feeling,' she said at last, 'that there are things between us here, that are destined to remain beyond your understanding.'

'Perhaps you could enlighten me.'

'Perhaps, or… perhaps like little bottles of poison, they have to be kept out of the reach of children.'

'And I'm the child, I suppose.'

'What I'm saying is,' she said, 'even if any of your assumptions were true, why would I say anything to *you*?'

'Because I can help you.'

'This would be the famous proposition. The one, no doubt, you're about to reveal.'

'Yes, but first I need to make something clear. This isn't coming from them. It's coming from me.'

I took a moment.

'I've decided to leave the Service,' I said.

Which was almost true. I hadn't quite *decided* to leave, but I was, it would be fair to say, giving it some serious consideration. I should add, and I say this with hindsight (oh yes, there it is again), this was more a case of giving *her* a chance to convince *me*, rather than the other way around. I was being reactive instead of proactive. But then again, I suppose that's what happens with these things. (I'm referring, of course, to that virus in my head. Encountering favourable conditions. Growing unchecked.)

'Is that so.'

I nodded, allowing the thought to sink in. She didn't believe me yet, not fully, but I could tell I'd piqued her interest.

'And I've come up with something that I think might work for both of us.'

'Keep going,' she said. 'I'm still waiting to hear how *you* can help *me*.'

'Well, for a start, I can continue to refrain from reporting in. That I've found you.'

She nearly said something, but seemed to think better of it.

'I could even put them off your scent. Throw out a false sighting. A chance, basically, is what I'm offering.'

'How much do you want?'

It took me a moment to realise what she meant.

'I don't want money,' I said. 'I'm not *blackmailing* you.'

'Why, then? Why would you do that?'

Why indeed.

'Let's just say you intrigue me.'

There was a pause, and she threw her head back and laughed.

'Now I've heard it all,' she said. 'I *intrigue* you!'

The kid at the next table was still staring at us. His mother was attempting to retrieve his attention.

'After one night in Bangkok,' she added with a smirk. 'Cute.'

'If you like.'

'So what exactly do you want from me? What do you want in return?

'I'm not asking for anything,' I said. 'Just... your honesty.'

She rightly scoffed at that. 'So that's your proposition, is it? My honesty for your silence.'

'Sure, why not? And my honesty too, I'll throw that in. Silence and honesty all round. How about that? We could continue where we left off.'

'Ah,' she said, nodding. 'Another night in Bangkok.'

'Or not. Whatever. We can just be friends, see what happens.'

'Sure,' she said. 'We can just be friends.'

'What's the downside? What have you got to lose? You can leave any time. Like you did in Bangkok. You'll still be free as a bird.'

She was thinking, really giving the idea her full attention, I could tell. Weighing up all the permutations.

'Free is good,' she said.

'It is.'

The breeze had picked up and a sudden gust rustled the surrounding palm trees.

'Well… *Jeff*… all I can say is, that's one hell of a proposition. And by that I mean, if I am who you say I am, you're taking one hell of a risk.'

'I am. A bit like you, perhaps? *Jasmine*? Meaning, even just coming here, to New Caledonia, a French territory… it seems to me you're taking a pretty big risk yourself. Maybe risk is your thing. Maybe danger turns you on.'

She didn't answer that. Perhaps she had no answer to it, perhaps I'd hit the nail on the head. She thought for a while, and then shook her head as if she couldn't quite get something straight.

'So you're leaving your job,' she said.

'That's right.'

'Quitting. Getting out. For good.'

I nodded.

'What are you going to do?'

I shrugged. 'It's time for a career change.'

'Not because of me.'

'Of course not.' Again, not a complete lie. It probably *was* time for a career change.

The family next to us noisily pushed their chairs out as they made to leave. The red-haired kid shot us a parting glance. Maybe he'll be a great fiction writer when he grows up.

'Tell me one thing,' she said. 'You say I intrigue you. You're not... *infatuated* with me, are you?'

'No,' I said, answering too quickly. 'Infatuated? Infatuated sounds a bit too much like obsessed. And to be honest, I'm not the type to be obsessed about anything.'

This of course *was* a lie, but she seemed to buy it. Almost. But not quite.

'Just a little bit,' she said. 'Just enough to be *intrigued*.'

'What's wrong with being intrigued?'

'What's wrong with it?' She looked at me, sizing me up. 'Susceptibility to being intrigued is a weakness.'

'That may be so. But we all have our vices.'

She scoffed at that. 'Vices. You have to grow up, you know? That's the thing, with life. That's the deal.'

'Sure. Of course it is. But you have to leave some space for poetic moments, too. And maybe this is one of mine.'

I let her think about that for a moment, and then added:

'After all... it's exhausting having to be sensible all the time. And maybe, don't you think, just a little bit boring?'

She donned her sunglasses again and looked down towards the beach, at the holidaymakers sunbathing and swimming. At the couples walking hand in hand. At least, that's what I saw – I'm not sure what she was looking at.

When she turned back to face me, her sunglasses remained firmly in place.

'You know what I think?' she said. 'I think you're lost. And you don't know who you are.'

'Really.'

'And *I* think…' She paused for a moment. 'I think you're trying to find yourself. And right now, weirdly, for whatever reason, maybe because I'm the nearest object of desire in that insulated life you must be leading, but right now you're trying to find yourself in *me*.'

It was me who stared at her this time. Where on earth did she get that from? I shook my head. After all, what else can you do, when the truth stares you in the face? Even if you don't realise it at the time.

'Look,' I managed to say eventually. 'I just think it might be fun.'

She smiled at me. It was as sly a smile as I've ever seen.

'Well now you put it that way,' she said.

She continued to smile. She looked relaxed.

She finished her coffee.

'OK,' she said. 'Now I have a proposition for *you*.'

Δ

A few hours later, just before 3pm, I was standing in the crowded main hall of Nouméa's city airport, and feeling decidedly on edge. I was waiting for Dala, and it was looking increasingly like she'd just done it again. I should have been kicking myself but I was ever the optimist.

35 minutes before departure: Still no sign. It was hardly surprising, but it wasn't as if I'd had a choice. Not given where my head was.

Her proposition back at Le Méridien had been an enticing one. She told me she'd already booked herself on a flight out of Nouméa that afternoon – the 3.30pm Air Calédonie flight to the Isle of Pines. It was only a half-hour flight away, but to escape the prying eyes of the local police (as sloppy as they were) it was always a good idea to keep moving. And the resort she was heading to was secluded. Did I want to join her? She'd test my 'honesty-for-honesty' proposal, and meet me at the airport. I was to buy a ticket for myself and wait for her. I'd have to trust her, just as she'd have to trust me.

20 minutes before departure: Boarding would be commencing shortly. The only question was whether I should fly there anyway, on the off-chance she'd turn up at the last minute. Or it might be like the train in Geneva, and perhaps I'd find her already on the plane in disguise.

After Le Méridien, I'd returned to my hotel. I'd had strict instructions: no phone calls, no deviations, just make my way back, grab my things, head straight to the airport alone, buy my ticket and sit tight. It was a test. And so as I say, what choice did I have? What would *you* have done in my place?

It was looking increasingly as if she'd done the obvious thing and simply packed her bags and caught a taxi to the international airport. She was probably on a plane somewhere over the Pacific by now, jetting off to who knew where.

18 minutes before departure: She turned up.

9.

Thursday, 14 October
Île des Pins (Isle of Pines),
New Caledonia

SHE WAS almost as beautiful asleep.

It was early the next morning. The tropical birdsong was already in full swing and the room was steadily growing lighter with the dawn. And as the rays of the newly risen sun began, gradually – one ray at a time – to pierce the surrounding forest canopy, I watched Dala as she slept. I'd been half-expecting her to be gone, and there I was, waking up in paradise.

The previous day, after Dala had surprised me and appeared like a wonderful apparition at the airport in Nouméa, we'd caught the short flight to the Isle of Pines, arriving at 4pm, just in time to catch the breathtaking colour of the water there – the most vibrant blue I'd ever seen that wasn't photo-enhanced. A bus trip later, we'd arrived at yet another resort. This one, though, was truly magical.

Surrounded by rainforest and white sand and warm, sapphire waters – and following us wherever we went, the twitter of birds and the faintly discernible sound of the ocean pounding the distant barrier reef – I'd found myself in a kind of heaven, only to be surpassed by a night of passion so intense, I was still incapable of processing it.

Our wild love affair had begun and I was, for now, entirely in the moment.

We had a stand-alone bungalow all to ourselves. Just about everything – the floors, the walls, the ceiling, the furniture – seemed to be dark brown and made of wood. And contrasting with that, our white sheets. And Dala. The sheet covering her – as if come to rest gently, like a layer of virgin snow – emphasized the graceful outline of her body: a muse's vision; a reclining Venus. Her hair – once blonde, now brown, and in this light, a vibrant bronze – was amassed on the pillow and her face wore a look of absolute peace: flawless honey-brown skin, sensuous, cocoa-coloured eyebrows, curving lips gently closed, her sleeping breath almost as silent as her cloistered dreams, sounding like the gentle waves washing up on the beach outside.

I couldn't imagine wanting to be anywhere else for any reason whatsoever.

Δ

Breakfast with Dala (those beautiful three words): we were sitting in the outdoor eating area under the palm trees, pool on one side, beach and inlet on the other, and in the distance, the surf-crowned reef and the open sea. We were late to arrive, and the other tables were by now only sparsely occupied. We'd finished our food – I'd eaten too much, the irresistible hazard of the buffet breakfast – and our coffee cups had already been refilled.

At one of the other tables sat a portly Caucasian male of Mediterranean appearance. He was wearing what could best be described as a parody of resort wear – brown sandals, white shorts, Hawaiian shirt, white panama with a black band – and he stood out. He was also making a poor attempt of disguising his frequent stares in our direction. If the weight of the evidence didn't suggest otherwise, I would have said he was spying on us. Literally. But for whom? I told myself I was being paranoid, although I could tell that Dala had clocked him as well.

'You don't think,' I said, keep one eye on the fat man, 'that you were taking a bit of a risk coming to a French territory?'

'You already said that.'

'You never answered.'

'I didn't know it was a question.' She then smiled and continued. 'Sure, there's *risk*. Whatever you do, there's *risk*. Maybe I like to do what no-one expects me to do. Maybe I like the feeling of being back in France without being back there, if you know what I mean. And I don't know, maybe I have that thing…. a subconscious wish to be caught?'

She grinned at me, a twinkle in her eye. I couldn't tell if she was teasing me.

'But you know,' she continued, 'the risk isn't as high as you might think.' She briefly glanced across at the fat man. 'You can see them coming for you here. The local police are hopeless and any Service people from France would stick out a mile.'

I lowered my voice. 'Do you think… the guy over there…?'

'No,' she said with a dismissive shake of her head.

We were silent for a moment.

'So,' I said, 'when you say you have a subconscious… wish…'

'Yes. Maybe I have a death wish.'

She looked at me in deadly earnest. Again, was she joking? I had no idea, but I gave her the benefit of the doubt.

'Something tells me you won't be dying before your time,' I said.

'*Pff*,' she scoffed. '"Before your time", such a stupid expression, you die when you die.'

And we left it at that.

A short time later our waiter for the morning, a friendly Kanak with a smile as warm as the midday sun, came over to clear away our empty coffee cups. It was time to begin to formulate a plan – a plan involving a likely choice between three locations: beach, pool, or bungalow. Meanwhile the fat man in the panama was still giving us at least fifty percent of his attention, a fact which may have played a role in what Dala said next.

'These places are bad for your health, I think.' She kept her voice down.

'You mean resorts? '

She nodded slowly. 'Yes. Resorts. I'm over them. I've *had my fill.*'

'I'm not surprised. Having said that… this *is* a rather good one, though, you have to admit.'

She tilted her head, signalling a lack of agreement.

'No volcano,' she said.

'No,' I replied, assuming she was joking, 'no volcano, that's true. You can't have everything.'

'But you can. You *can* have everything.' And then she added: 'We should go.'

'We should.' I looked at my watch. 'Fancy a swim? Or is it too early?'

'No I mean… we should leave here. Leave the island.'

'We just got here!' I protested. A little too loudly. The fat man would have approved, although I noticed he was in the process of upping stumps: he'd just stood up and was shuffling away.

'Let's go to Tanna,' she said.

'Where?'

'Tanna. It's an island in Vanuatu. Supposed to be amazing. It has a volcano. And you can sleep in a treehouse and listen to the rumbles and booms.'

'The rumbles and booms. What is it with you and volcanoes?'

'I love volcanoes. Always have.'

'And they obviously love you, too. After that ash cloud.'

'You mean the ash cloud that saved me from you?' she

asked, with that twinkle in her eye again.

In all seriousness. How could I have said no?

Δ

Needless to say, I was completely smitten at this point. Now, even though I was heavily 'under the influence' and was barely able to see past the next hour let alone the next month, I wasn't yet so far gone I'd forgotten I had a job.

It did occur to me, given I'd been toying with the idea anyway, and given how far I'd taken this, that I should resign. To save a little bit of self-respect, if nothing else. But the truth of the matter is I couldn't bring myself to speak to Alan. Not then, not in the middle of it all.

So I pushed it to the back of my mind – back into the far, dark recesses – and told myself I'd deal with it later. Because anyway, who knew what might happen in the meantime. There could be an asteroid strike, or a nuclear war. Or a volcanic cataclysm.

10.

SHE TURNED to face me and smiled, her face aglow in the morning light.

We'd flown into Nouméa earlier that morning following our idyllic two-night stay on the Isle of Pines, enjoyed a pleasant fifty-kilometre taxi ride through the countryside, and had just arrived at the international airport in plenty of time to catch our Air Vanuatu flight to Port Vila. I can still remember that moment in front of the airport entrance when she stopped and turned to face me. It was as if Time had stood still, as if the universe had paused, just to allow me to savour what was before me, what the heavens, what Life, had sent me.

And how, I ask you, could I not have loved that face? Her eyes, the colour of the turquoise waters of the island we'd just come from, were shining and happy. Her smile was as bright as the tropical days ahead of us. As far as I knew.

'So,' she said. 'Jeff. Our first overseas trip together.'

'It is, Jasmine. Although not our first trip over the sea.'

'That is true. And may there be many more.'

May there be many more. She actually said that.

Δ

It occurred to me – at around this point, just as we were walking into the airport – that it might be a bad idea, from my perspective, for us to be travelling together. At least internationally, with all the border and security checks. Even though we were travelling as Jasmine Carroll and Jeff Perry on our false French and Canadian passports, I realised this could come back to bite me later, should Dala's fake passport come to the attention of my employers. My own fake identity was, after all, lovingly created by them, and it might make for an uncomfortable conversation were I to be asked why I happened to be travelling with the person I was claiming I couldn't find. Clearly, we had to split up, at least until we were through customs in Port Vila.

You couldn't be too careful in this business.

Δ

'Jasmine.'

'Yes, Jeff?'

We'd just entered the main hall, with a view to finding our check-in counter. I steered Dala over to one side, pretending to look for travel documents. Next to an indoor

79

palm tree, I told her my fears. Said we should split up from this point, check in separately, and catch up again in Port Vila. And I don't think it was wishful thinking when I thought I detected a fleeting, deflated look. Of course, she said, it's good idea. Her carefree face soon returned though, and I suspect the extra precaution probably served to remind her of the constant presence of one of her favourite things: danger.

She even said to me in a playful tone:

'You want to hear a little secret of mine? When you're travelling, you know where the best hiding place is?'

'Buried in dirty underwear.'

'Really? No, in your heel. The heel of your shoe. But never in airports, or on planes, not these days, with all the attention shoes get. Always taking them off, getting them scanned. But away from airports? The only time I've ever had someone insist on properly checking my shoes was a dumb cop in Brazil, and even then he didn't find the compartment.'

'You have a compartment in those?' I asked. She was wearing her Havaianas flip-flops.

'No, stupid! In shoes, and I told you, not in airports.'

'So, in your heel? I'll remember that when I'm feeling nosey.'

'When we get to Vanuatu,' she said, speaking softly into my ear, 'you can be as nosey as you like.'

'I may have to take you up on that.'

'Do what you have to do.'

At which point she kissed me – passionately, pushing her body into mine and grabbing my buttocks at the same time – before disengaging, winking, and turning away. I watched her for a few moments as she marched away towards the check-in counter. I stayed put, pretending to look at my phone: I thought I'd give her a couple of minutes before joining the queue.

She barely left, though – she was back in seconds. From the look on her face, everything had changed.

She came up close and spoke to the floor.

'*Police.* Everywhere.' There was venom in her voice – she spoke like a different person.

I looked up and saw what she meant. Apart from a roaming pair doing the usual rounds, there was a large group of police – maybe six or seven of them – over near a service desk. Thankfully none of them seemed to be looking in our direction, and their presence was loudly advertised, so it didn't feel like a bust. On the other hand, they didn't look like they were here simply to bolster airport security either. An awful thought occurred to me: the fat man at the resort – had he overheard our plans to fly to Vanuatu?

I looked at Dala. Her face said it all, a mixture of anger and hurt. Before she uttered a word, I realised she thought I'd betrayed her.

'Did you?' she asked.

'No, D… No. I didn't.'

'You wanted to split up. Is this why?'

'No. I swear.'

She looked into my eyes for a moment. I didn't know if I'd passed, but it didn't feel like I'd failed either. With Dala, of course, you could never really tell.

'Do you think you've been spotted somewhere?' I asked. 'At the resort maybe? On the Isle Of Pines?'

She surveyed the hall again, making a million intuitive calculations in seconds.

'I don't know. It's possible,' she said, and then looked at me. 'We don't have much choice, though. The sooner we get out of here the better.'

'I agree.'

'But we do it together. No splitting up.'

And there it was. The hard bargain. Prove yourself, she was saying. As cover for her, we had to stay together. For her sake, not mine. Her chances improved with a travelling companion; mine – with this companion in particular – most certainly worsened. I should have been as hard-nosed as her. I should have said no.

'OK,' I said.

It did occur to me, even at the time, that there I was, crossing another line. That helping her in this way would make me even more complicit than I already was. I realised, in other words, that I'd just taken another of those dangerous little steps.

So we joined the queue at the check-in counter. Out of the corner of my eye, I watched the police. If it was us they were after, and they'd seen us – and recognized us – then they were holding back. Possibly waiting for the customs check.

We checked in – we were allocated adjoining seats – and made our way to the customs queue.

We tried to 'act natural', to look like happy tourists. We should have been trying to look like honeymooners, but for me at least it was hard enough keeping the look of tension out of my face. Dala, too, I could tell, was feeling it. You'd think she'd have been pretty used to this sort of thing by now, but clearly not.

We reached the head of the queue and waited for the nod from the customs officer. When we got it, we approached together. Melanesians must be one of the most friendly peoples on earth, with customs officers among the least, so a combination is always interesting. Sometimes you'll be greeted with a smile, sometimes you won't. Today, we weren't.

The officer took our passports, and looked at them gravely, from one to the other. He kept looking up at Dala.

'Mademoiselle Jasmine Carroll,' he announced grandly, flicking through the pages of Dala's passport.

Dala kept her cool, smiled, said nothing.

The officer looked up, caught her smile and then threw a glance over our shoulders. In the direction of the police officers.

'I remember you,' he said, speaking in French.

He seemed to be hoping for a reaction.

'I never forget a face,' he added, with a smile. So we got our smile, just not the right type.

'Mademoiselle Jasmine Carroll,' he repeated. 'From

Paris, France. I stamped your passport when you arrived.'

'Ah, yes…' Dala said, pretending it was coming back to her and turning on the charm. 'I remember…'

'Except when you arrived, you were alone.'

He'd turned cold, rebuffing Dala's friendliness and, I assumed, quelling his inner Melanesian. He let the statement hang there in the brittle air-conditioned air for a moment, continuing to ignore me and stare at Dala. If there had been any doubt before, there could be none now. He was suspicious. He had been from the moment he saw her – perhaps there was an alert out. If so, she was going to need more than a change of hair colour to save her. Her eyes, for one thing – her luminous, blue-green eyes – were just as beautiful, just as conspicuous as ever. I desperately wanted to look around to see what the police were doing, but I didn't dare.

'It's a little bit strange, don't you think?' he continued. 'You arrive alone, you leave with someone.'

'I got lucky,' she said with a theatrical wink. It didn't work. He remained visibly brimming with scepticism.

'Is that so,' he said, his attention shifting from Dala to his computer screen. He began to tap away at his keyboard.

Manufacturing my best chuckle, and in fluent French, I piped in:

'My wife's joking. We flew in separately, I was detained at work.'

The key-tapping stopped. He looked at me.

'Your wife?'

I nodded. 'De facto wife. We live together in Paris.'

For the first time, he looked troubled. Examined our passports again, laboriously, especially mine. And then, it would appear, after much soul-searching and with a considerable degree of reluctance, he eventually threw in the proverbial towel.

After sighing deeply, he aggressively stamped our passports with two loud *thwonkers* and handed them back, his joyless face as wooden as a Kanak statue.

We were through.

Δ

I tried not to think too hard about what role, if any, I may have played in Dala's escape from New Caledonia. It was easy enough to tell myself – and so I did – that she could handle herself perfectly well on her own and didn't need any help from me. And anyway, I had plenty to distract me from such thoughts. A day of island-hopping, for one thing.

We arrived in Port Vila at lunchtime – involving a far more relaxed customs experience, as it turned out – before flying on to Tanna that afternoon. The Isle Of Pines, Grande Terre (Nouméa), Efate (Port Vila) and Tanna: four Coral Sea islands in a day was enough to make a person forget almost anything. And when you're lucky enough to be accompanied by a woman like Dala… well, need I say more?

11.

Friday, 15 October to
Thursday, 11 November
Mount Yasur, Tanna, Vanuatu

SHE CRIED out in unabashed delight.

When we peered over the edge of the crater rim for the
first time, catching a glimpse of the small, bright, lava lake
in the pit far below, and felt, as much as heard, the awe-
inspiring, bone-shaking reports, emanating, it seemed, from
the very depths of the Earth itself, I was as transfixed by
Dala's wide-eyed excitement as I was by the spectacle before
us. This recollection has a CinemaScope clarity for me still –
aural as well as visual – and stands out among the vivid store
of my memories from this period when we were together. I
can still hear the volcano's thunderous detonations, they
never leave my head. The mountain, in a way, was like Dala:
untamed, unpredictable, and ultimately unknowable.

After flying into Tanna, we caught a ride in a four-wheel

drive across the island to our accommodation in the shadow of Mount Yasur, one of the most active volcanoes in the world. For almost four weeks we stayed, not in a resort, but in a tree house, nestled in a banyan tree, from where we could hear the continuous 'rumbles and booms' and see the orange glow at night that was sometimes bright enough to form eerie patterns on the wall of our room: silhouettes of jungle leaves.

What did we do all that time exactly? It's difficult for me to remember now. When you're completely at peace with the world, and everything is in perfect equilibrium, it's hard to focus on the details. Time was an irrelevance. There was food, there was sex, there were the deepest of deep sleeps. There were volcano visits and arousing swims. Steamy heat and evening thunderstorms. The sound of raindrops slapping into flat, sheltering leaves, and the constant echo of a myriad sonatas of bird calls sounding across the expanse of perpetual twilight beneath the forest canopy.

What did we do? All I know is, these were the happiest days of my life. Twenty-seven perfect, blissful days. But don't ask me to account for them, I noted down nothing, kept no diary. What would've been the point? How do you describe happiness?

I gave no thought to Alan or to my job. I had no idea, and nor did I care, whether or not questions were being asked. Whether I was now, officially, an intelligence officer lost in the South Pacific. Whether I was the first. (I'll wager I wasn't.)

There are four things I recall in particular from our time there, living in that tree house. That first visit to the volcano is one of those things.

The second thing happened on a visit much later, I've no idea when. But like the first time, it was late afternoon and the light was seductive. We were again on the crater rim, watching the show, but this time Dala was strangely silent. And then she suddenly turned and hugged me, held me close. She kissed my cheek and whispered into my ear.

'I love you,' she said.

The third thing is a conversation. One evening over a few drinks I asked her again about what happened in the Alps. She'd always, up until then, been adamant that her life as a French operative was a no-go area, including why she left them, and why she'd apparently betrayed them. That evening though, she opened up to me a little. It was a terrible accident, she told me, and anyway, the whole thing had been her associate's idea, not hers. She'd argued against it. And yet, even so, the death of the woman was something that still weighed on her heavily. She'd never got over it, and never would. I asked her why she was so hard on herself when she'd obviously done all she could in the circumstances. She responded by asking me, in turn, whether I'd ever felt responsible, collectively or otherwise, for someone's death. I said I couldn't say I had.

'Sometimes' she said, 'I just want to go to the most dangerous place in the world, and lay myself open to the worst it can throw at me. It's as if this pain, I need to burn it away. To… what's the word? To cauterize it.'

Despite this confession, she wouldn't tell me who she'd been acting for, and I accepted that it was not something she was willing to go into. That was just how it was: I had to take her as I found her – this person before me, living with me, sleeping with me – and not judge her for the person she may have once been, or for her past mistakes. And I could relate to that, I even privately applauded it. Because, after all, I'd made mistakes too. And so I acquiesced in this unspoken demand of hers.

And because I loved her.

Which brings me to the fourth thing. I decided to ask her to marry me. Or if marriage wasn't her thing, to at least make our relationship more permanent in some overt way, such as buy a place somewhere – or a yacht, if that worked better – and make a home together. As delirious and half-baked as it sounds now – this idea that we might get married – it seemed at the time the most natural thing in the world. Rapid, yes, but not impetuous. Just an obvious, logical progression. As for my life before Dala, I told myself it was simply a case of that was then, and this was now. Marrying her was never a concept I had to wrestle with, not in the slightest.

I never got around to asking her though.

12.

SHE WAS the one who suggested it.

It was supposed to have been a short break from the somewhat spartan amenities of the tree house. A few nights in a resort on the other side of the island. It was fine as far as I was concerned. It was *all* fine.

And so, after twenty-seven days and twenty-eight nights in our little paradise, we returned to the island's western shore on the twelfth of November, a Friday. We checked into a place called the White Grass Ocean Resort and quickly took advantage of the luxury on offer in one of the bungalows there. A large, comfortable bed. Manicured gardens and wide, ocean views, the Coral Sea at our doorstep. I, for one, had no complaints, it was a delightful change. I didn't, however, foresee what was about to happen.

The next day, Saturday, after snorkelling in the deep rock pools in front of the resort, we had lunch in the restaurant. We sat at a small table next to the open-air window, and enjoyed a view across the lawn to the sea. There was a pleasant breeze, and over the low-level lunchtime clamour and clatter, you could hear the persistent sound of gentle swells breaking against the reef at the bottom of the garden.

It soon became clear, though, that all was not well. We'd only just sat down when Dala complained of an upset stomach. She told me not to worry, to go ahead with my meal without her. She insisted that I take my time, saying that she'd have a short nap. And so I did, enjoying the change of scenery and the delicious, well-earned lunch. I had a book with me, and it was possibly an hour before I made it back to our bungalow.

Dala was nowhere to be seen.

Nor, I soon realised, were her clothes, or her toiletries. Her suitcase wasn't there either. In fact everything of hers had gone, except for an envelope with her handwriting on the front. It was addressed to me – that is, to Jeff. Inside was a note which began with 'Dear Jeff' and ended with 'Love J' and it was impossible not to pick up the references to the Dear Jasmine note I'd left her at the hotel in Nouméa. The note read:

> *Dear Jeff. Fish slipped net. Swimming to where they speak its language. Will miss duologues with fisherman. Love J.*

The resort was near the airport, close enough to see the planes flying past low over the sea. It was 2.45pm when I dialled Reception but I knew the answer before they told me: the next scheduled departure, the 2.50pm flight to Port Vila, was the last for the day. The next flight wasn't until 11.50am the following morning.

All I had to do was step outside and walk down to the bottom of the garden, and I could wave her goodbye.

It felt like Paris all over again. Paris and Bangkok, rolled into one. I cursed myself, told myself I must have known, even before that final morning together, that she was never going to trust me, or anyone, for that matter. I noted it was a month to the day since this adventure had begun back at our rendezvous at Le Méridien in Nouméa. Had she planned it that way? I wondered. Was overrunning a month breaking some secret rule of hers?

But then I thought about something that had happened the night before. We were having dinner. She was gazing at me – there was a strange look in her eyes – and she held her stare for longer than felt natural. Even at the time I wondered what it was that she was thinking, or was about to say. Of course, in light of subsequent events, I now realised that it must have been somehow connected with her decision to leave me. More than that though – there'd been a softness, a warmth in those blue-green eyes that evening – I felt it was a sign that I almost managed to hold on to her.

Almost.

13.

Friday, 28 October 2011
Mount Nyiragongo,
Democratic Republic Of Congo

'SHE IS pure beauty, this one.'

At Fabien's words, as if in response, the ground trembled. Steam once again began hissing out of vents near the crater rim.

At the base of the crater, the lava lake was becoming even more agitated, even more alive, as it heaved and churned, and rolled into itself. On the surface of the lake, refulgent, pomegranate-red lava was bubbling and splattering up and out between the bending, shifting, dark slabs of liquid rock – black plates separated by jigsaw cracks of bright orange – and the whole tableau was a tumbling, morphing, ever-changing spectacle, accompanied by a steady, building roar, like a passing squadron of MiG-21s.

Mount Nyiragongo (elevation 3,470 m / 11,384 ft), is

located in the DRC near the border of Rwanda, about fifteen kilometres north of the city of Goma, and is, like Mount Yasur, one of the world's most active volcanoes. And the most dangerous, with its pyroclastic surges, poisonous gases, suffocating ash and pulverising bombs of molten rock. Even the lava in motion is lethal: in a recent eruption, lava flows careering down the side of the mountain reached speeds of up to sixty kilometres an hour, the fastest ever observed.

It also holds the world's largest lava lake, and that's what Fabien and I were looking down upon, from high up on Nyiragongo's crater rim. There was a cold sharp wind blowing and an all-pervading smell of sulphur – an inescapable, acrid reek of rotten eggs and gunpowder. With all this fire and brimstone, the day felt biblical.

'She is pure beauty,' Fabien repeated, in his heavy French accent. He liked to practise his English on me, and somewhere along the line he'd seized upon that old-fashioned penchant for using the feminine pronoun when referring to inanimate objects (in French, volcano is masculine: *le volcan*).

'She is,' I said, but without sincerity. Beauty, as far as I was concerned, was nowhere to be seen.

Speaking of which…

It had been almost a year since Dala left me in Vanuatu, and circumstances had conspired to deliver me to the heart of Africa and this most formidable of vantage points. The man standing beside me, Fabien, was a member of a team of French volcanologists on an expedition to Nyiragongo.

Their ultimate aim was to better understand, and thus predict, the volcano's notoriously violent eruptions – something of critical importance to the citizens of greater Goma: at least a million people lived directly in the firing line of the mountain's wrath. I had been keen to join them – I had my reasons – and had managed to wangle an invitation to tag along as both an assistant and an observer.

Fabien and I were both keeping a wary eye on Nicolas, a member of the team, as he abseiled down the crater wall. Other expedition members – I could see Thierry, Cédric, Bruno and Virginie – were standing further along the crater rim directly above Nicolas, and were looking on anxiously as well. Huddled together further away again were a number of our African porters and two guards – all of them from Goma – and they, no less than the volcanologists, were keenly scrutinizing the first stage of the team's exploration of the volcano's crater and its scene-stealing lava lake. Everything about this place was a contradiction: there was the visual contrast of the grey-black rock against the crimson glow of the magma, and there was the confusion of physical sensations with the cold from the altitude and the rarefied air competing with the warmth emanating from the volcano beneath our feet.

'The locals believe that this is where all things evil must come to die,' said Fabien. 'But I think the opposite is true. I think this is where *beauty* comes to die.'

A hundred metres below us, the abseiling volcanologist continued his tentative descent. Securely fastened to a rope, he was making his way down to a newly formed 'splatter cone' to collect lava samples.

He stopped, apparently to check something. And then, hesitantly, as if he wasn't sure why he was doing it, he turned and looked up at the members of his team above him. Perhaps he'd been meaning to get someone to send him down his portable spectrometer to analyse the gas releases, or perhaps it was a premonition, but whatever the reason, it was lucky for him he looked up. Because at that precise moment, a chunk of rock the size of a minivan dislodged itself above where he was standing. His reflexes were good: he dropped what he'd been holding and leapt to one side, a course of action which lost him his lava pick but saved his life.

Δ

Despite the passing of a year since Dala's departure, not a day had gone by without me thinking about her. Maybe not even an hour, as disconcerting as that sounds.

From the outset, I couldn't get that note out of my head.

Dear Jeff. Fish slipped net. Swimming to where they speak its language. Will miss duologues with fisherman. Love J.

I went over it ad nauseam. Looking for hidden meanings, agonising over it.

What did she mean, 'to where they spoke her language'? Was I to take it literally, meaning to somewhere French-speaking? Surely not. Surely she meant it metaphorically, to somewhere more her style. And so what was that? What was more her style? She'd told me she wanted to go to the most dangerous place in the world, to 'cauterize the pain'. Was that what she meant?

Was I to take the message as a scalding rejection? Yet she said in the message that she will miss our 'duologues', which brought to mind the look on her face the night before she left me. Despite the message, despite her actions, I knew she had strong feelings for me.

Fish slipped net. Did this indicate a fear of being betrayed? Did she never fully trust me? What if, before it was too late, I'd proposed to her? Might that have made a difference? Again, all I could think of was that warm look in her eyes when she'd stared at me over dinner. Any regret that she was feeling at the time was now overshadowed by my own, because all I could think of were the things I should have done. What if, if only.

Perhaps there was something she couldn't tell me? Maybe for my own good? An approaching danger? Or perhaps it was a test. Did she want me to attempt to follow her? To test my mettle?

It was impossible to draw a conclusion. The only thing I knew was that it left me with no choice. Because no matter what the message meant, I needed to know. To know which it was, a rejection, or a test, or a cry for help.

I knew I was going to have to find her, in other words, no matter what it took.

Δ

After his near-death experience, Nicholas began making his way back up the crater wall with a view to rejoining the team.

Clearly he'd had enough excitement for one day.

Fabien and I continued to observe the volcanologist's slow vertical progress. I could feel the pulsing heat from the lava lake below and I was about to comment on it when there was a sudden, heart-stopping explosion. It came from the lava lake. An eruption of lava – one thousand degrees hot – arced into the natural stadium in front of us, the gigantic globs dispersing and cooling as they rose and fell, as if in slow motion, and splattering on the crater floor below.

I breathed an expletive. Fabien and the other volcanologists hooted, now sufficiently recovered, apparently, after having observed the near annihilation of their colleague.

It never stopped, this beast. This aggressor. On any view of it, danger was all around us. The rockfalls, the lava bombs, the deadly carbon dioxide emissions, at any moment you could be killed in a place like this. On the one hand I was intrigued by the heroism – or foolhardiness – that was clearly a prerequisite to being a volcanologist, and on the other I wanted to get as far away from these daredevils and their mountain as quickly as humanly possible. I just couldn't figure out how to do it without losing face.

After stopping to keep an eye on the lava lake for a moment, Nicolas continued his ascent. I was pleased I wasn't where he was, but not pleased I wasn't back in Goma.

'This volcano,' I said to my companion, 'would you say it's the most... hazardous you've been on?'

Fabien, who was swarthy with short black hair and bald on top, gave me one of those French half-shrugs – with the jutting lower jaw, the downturned mouth –as he surveyed the subject of my question.

'She is hazardous, that is true. Very hazardous, very dangerous. But, you know, the people are *more* dangerous.'

'The people?'

'Sure, the people.' Fabien turned to glance at the Africans. 'You see those guards over there? Carrying their guns, their AK-47s? They are carrying them for a reason, no? The people they are protecting us from, *those* people, they are the big danger around here. In this part of the world, you are more likely to be killed by a bullet than a lava bomb.'

'So you mean the rebels? The militia groups?'

'The militia groups, the army, the… how do you say it… rogue… the rogue soldiers. Even the police.'

'The police?'

'Around here, it is better not to pick sides. Better to just get in, get out. You know? Never mind the volcano. She is a sweetheart compared to them.'

Δ

After Dala had left me that terrible Saturday at the White Grass Ocean Resort, and after I'd finished agonising over the note and made my decision to find her again come what may, there remained a further issue to resolve: there was still the delicate but pressing question of what to do with the job that I presumably still held, however undeservedly.

Clearly, even if doing my job and notifying my employer of Dala's movements was something I was willing to do, the time for so doing had well and truly passed. Or it certainly had if I wanted to avoid the sack, and it probably had if I wanted to avoid being arrested. In Bangkok, and then in New Caledonia and Vanuatu, I'd disobeyed orders, crossed line after line, and enmeshed myself in a conflict of interest that was nigh on inescapable and would damn me to hell if it ever saw the light of day. Not to mention the small matter of helping an internationally sought-after fugitive to flee a jurisdiction, which had to have been a criminal offence in someone's book, somewhere. If not in everyone's book, everywhere.

Equally though, and for all the same reasons, I couldn't see how I could carry on working as an intelligence officer with the SIS. Not with all the excess baggage. Simply put, handing in my notice had become my only way forward.

I figured I could do without the salary payments that had, despite my failure to report in, still been landing punctually in my bank account. I could live cheaply, and survive by dipping into my nest egg as needed. After all, I was already paying for my own expenses: I'd stopped submitting my hotel bills ever since I'd gone off-piste after arriving in Nouméa. I'd have to let go of my flat in London, a modest studio flat in Ladbroke Grove – it had been leased to me fully furnished, with the rent paid for by my employer. But it would be easy to let go of: I had only meagre possessions, and there was nothing there of any value or meaning to me.

This option had the added advantage of enabling me to continue my search for Dala with a clean conscience. It had already occurred to me that resigning might help salvage some self-respect – or whatever was left of it – and it was never too late to do that.

Furthermore, by leaving the Service, I'd be keeping the promise I made to Dala. In attempting to convince her of my sincerity, I'd told her I was leaving because it was time for a career change, and it probably was. But what has become clear to me now, is that a big influence on this decision of mine to actually go through with it and quit was the thought that when I ran into Dala again, I'd be able to tell her that I'd done it, that I was no longer the face of the enemy but a free agent at last. I'd persuaded myself, I think, that my failure to resign earlier had been the thing that had ultimately driven her away. And that by finally following through on my promise, it might somehow be enough.

And so, still at the resort on Tanna, I summoned the strength to ring Alan. I knew that he wouldn't let me go easily and mentally prepared myself to deal with that.

When I dialled his number and waited for him to pick up, to my ear the insistent beeping of the ringing tone sounded more like a sonorous death knell.

After an eternity, he answered. Or should I say pressed the green button on his phone, he was never the first to speak when called. And he always knew who it was, so there was no reason to identify yourself. Or engage in pleasantries: other than the occasional reference to the weather, he disliked small talk in phone conversations. So I got straight down to it. No point in beating around the bush.

'In advance,' I said into the silence, 'I'd like to apologise for any inconvenience this might cause you, and if there was any other way I could in all good conscience do this, I would.' It sounded rehearsed – which it was – but it was the best I could do.

'Sounds ominous,' he said, in a tone that was precisely that. 'You realise it's pouring here. And cold. This doesn't sound like the ray of sunshine that's going to brighten up my miserable autumn day.'

'No I don't think it will.'

'I was hoping you were going to tell me you'd finally found her.'

'The opposite, I'm afraid.'

'Meaning?'

'Meaning I'm handing in my resignation.'

There was a long pause.

'You mean you're *offering* to resign,' he said eventually.

'I'm offering to resign, yes.'

'Why?'

'You know… Time for a change, and all that.'

Another pause.

'When we last met,' he began, '… in June I believe… so, what, four months ago… I suggested to you back then that you might be well-served by taking your annual leave early.'

'You did.'

'And I'd like to repeat that suggestion now.'

'And I appreciate that,' I said. 'I really do. But it's not about needing a holiday. It's the work. It's the job.'

'*And*... as I said in June, we can move you. Get you off the case, as it were.'

'Thank you... but no thank you. I've made up my mind. I need a career change.'

'Don't we all. Or don't we all think we do. All of us, we all go through this. It's completely normal... no, it's *par for the course* in a job like ours. At least take that break, give it a few weeks and reconsider your position then.'

'Thank you, as I say, but I really have made up my mind.

Another pause, but this one felt uglier somehow.

'I'm not sure I'm inclined to accept your offer to resign,' he said with an air of finality – it wasn't an invitation to dissuade him, it was the announcement of a decision.

I'd been expecting this. It was time to bring out, albeit reluctantly, my excuse of last resort. The big guns.

'I have to be honest with you,' I said, employing that alternative definition of *honest* that appears in no dictionary. 'I didn't want to say anything, I was too ashamed, but... I've had a crisis. A kind of... nervous breakdown I guess. Anxiety, depression. No sleep. *Drinking*'s off the scale, Christ. My evenings are... And it's not just the evenings.' I paused, to let that last one sink in. 'I'm a mess, simple as that. It's driven me over the edge, this job. I'm sorry, but I'm not cut out for it.'

I waited for Alan to respond but there was only silence. I sensed he didn't fully believe me, but I forged on:

'So this is no spur of the moment thing, I assure you. I certainly haven't taken this decision lightly. I've agonized over it, absolutely… torn myself apart. It really is best for everyone. I'm sorry. You've been good to me. Given me every chance.'

More silence and I waited, sitting this one out. Alan eventually spoke.

'No need to apologise. All of us, we do what we have to do. And you're no exception.'

I couldn't help but hear a brutal emphasis on that last sentence.

'Very well,' he continued. 'All that remains to be done then is for you to return the document we provided you with…' (meaning my fake Canadian passport) '… and you'll have to follow the usual procedure or else we'll be forced to come and get you.'

The 'usual procedure' involved a confirmation in writing containing somewhere a special code word – there was a word confirming the truth of the statement and another alerting the recipient that the sender is under duress.

'I will,' I said. 'And again, I have to say—'

But he was gone.

I have to confess, the sadness of the moment took me by surprise. (Goodbye Alan, so long Jeff Perry.) While I should have been elated, I felt only emptiness. Still, I knew I had a job to do, and I immediately set about doing it.

Δ

Nicolas, the abseiler, finally reached the crater rim. The oldest member of the team, he was a fit forty-five-year-old:

lithe, with the sharp muscle-definition of a gymnast, the craggy face of experience and, on most days, a friendly smile. There was not much of a smile now though, just a look of exhaustion, both physical and emotional. He was clearly shaken up.

Two of the other members, Bruno and Cédric, helped him scramble up onto what must have been for him the welcome relief of solid ground at last.

I knew all about the yearning for solid ground.

Δ

Finding Dala again proved to be far more difficult this time. There were no leads, every chain of inquiry drew a complete blank. It didn't matter how many times I tried to place myself in her shoes, how many times I tried to think like her, it all led nowhere and came to nothing. It was as though she'd vanished off the face of the earth. The months rolled by.

After such a long and fruitless search, most people in my position would have simply given up. Chalked it up to experience, moved on. But the fact that I'd failed to unearth any useful information whatsoever only made me more determined: I'd never been the type to give up easily, not once I'd set my mind to it – I'd carry it through to the bitter end, whatever the task, let alone something as important as finding the woman I'd been on the verge of proposing to. And so I decided to try a new tack.

I decided to try to get my old job back.

I realised I'd have a better chance of finding Dala with the SIS's resources behind me. I'd beg, I'd grovel. I'd say I was fully recovered and plead with them to put me back on the SANDPIPER case, arguing the pool of knowledge I'd built up would be invaluable. And even if the job of tracking down Dala was no longer open to me, I'd still be able to access the Service's extensive range of contacts and intel, to conduct a little enquiry of my own on the side.

It failed though, this great plan of mine. I didn't even manage to make it past first base. Alan stonewalled me, neither accepting nor returning any of my many calls. He treated me as if I was nothing more than a slightly unhinged member of the general public out to waste his time – which, when you look at it, was pretty much what I was. Similarly, my formal application to re-apply was met with an equally formal rejection, no reasons given. I managed to find out through one of my ex-colleagues in the Service that I was no longer seen as having the right character for the job. I could hardly blame them, given my colourful performance in that last phone call to Alan.

And so I kept searching on my own. I assured myself that without my job I'd be directionless anyway, and that the travel would help me refocus.

As the days, weeks and months continued to tick over, my determination to find her only grew stronger. I did wonder if I was becoming addicted to the chase, though. This thought bothered me, but didn't stop me. Nor did the thought that without my career as an intelligence officer, finding Dala had become my sole purpose, my raison d'être – after all, there were plenty of purposes far worse. But it did occur to me that it was almost as if she'd come to define me, in my own mind. This in turn brought to mind her comment, at Le Méridien in Nouméa, that I was lost and didn't know who I was, and that I was trying to find myself in her.

I hadn't given it much consideration at the time, but thinking about it now, in the middle of this mad search for her, it did make me wonder: could she have been right?

Δ

'That was a close shave,' I said.

I'd wandered over to have a word to Nicolas. He'd shed his abseiling gear and was taking a few moments to get his breath back.

'A close…?'

Like Fabien, the other volcanologists, including Nicolas, preferred that I speak to them in English so they could hone their linguistic skills. It was a tad annoying, as my French was far better than their English, but I obliged because I felt I owed them.

'A lucky escape,' I clarified. 'It was very close.'

He stared down into the crater for a few moments. I wondered if he was still in shock, wondered if I should fetch Thierry, the team doctor.

'It was close,' he said finally, with the red glow of the lava lake reflected in his eyes. 'But… I am not sure if it was so lucky.'

'Yes, you did well. Quick reaction.'

'No, I mean, I think it is not so lucky to have a close escape. You only get a certain number and today I used up another one.'

I nodded sympathetically, seeing his point.

'And anyway,' he added. 'I lost my pick. It is very bad luck to lose your pick.'

Δ

I finally got the break I'd been looking for.

It had been almost a year since Dala had left me. Ever since my resignation, and especially since my subsequent failure to make any headway, I'd been quietly hounding my ex-colleagues at the SIS for any piece of information they could throw my way. I was careful to convey the impression I was simply asking out of professional curiosity – out of an eagerness to learn the outcome of the case I'd been working on when I left. Understandably perhaps, they nevertheless remained fairly tight-lipped, but all I needed was one tasty morsel. And that's exactly what I got.

I found out that a postcard from Dala to an old friend in Paris had been intercepted. I was spared the details – where the postcard was sent from, or what was written on it – but was reliably informed that it hinted at her either being in, or having recently been in, East Africa. In Kigali, to be precise, the capital of Rwanda.

I was in South Korea at the time – so not even close – and immediately booked the flights necessary to get me to

Kigali. Once there, and after a lot of asking around, I managed to coax a priceless tip-off out of a bar manager who I sensed had taken a bit of a shine to her (he was only human). He'd organised Dala's transport across the border into the DRC. To Goma.

Goma. Arguably the most dangerous city in the world, with Mount Nyiragongo on one side and the methane-and-carbon-dioxide-laden Lake Kivu on the other, threatening a catastrophic overturn – a 'limnic eruption' – at any time. Not to mention the region's brutal conflicts, the endless civil wars.

Goma. Slap-bang in the middle of an area riven with smuggling, warfare and volcanism; replete with riches, cruelty and mortal danger. It made sense. Given what she'd said about going somewhere to cauterize the pain, it was perfectly logical that she'd be drawn to the least-safe city on the least-safe continent. French-speaking too, so it was a place that spoke her language both metaphorically *and* literally.

Goma. I really should have guessed it.

And so I made my way there, and in that city in the shadow of a volcano, I continued my enquiries. And an idea occurred to me.

Mount Nyiragongo isn't the only active volcano near Goma, it's just the closest. Not much further away, for example, there's Mount Nyamuragira, and both are located in the Virunga Mountains, a chain of active and dormant volcanoes located near the conjunction of the borders of the

DRC, Rwanda and Uganda. There are volcanoes everywhere.

And so I posed as someone interested in volcanoes. Why not? When I thought about it, volcanoes were central to everything about Dala: there was the ash cloud that had enabled her escape from Europe; there was her patent predilection for them, as evidenced by the book she'd been reading in the library in Nouméa and by her own admission (*I love volcanoes, always have*); and then of course there was Mount Yasur on Tanna where I'd spent the happiest weeks of my life. And there I was, in the volcano capital of the world. It was a line of enquiry worth pursuing.

Which was how I came across my team of French volcanologists. With a couple of lies and a load of enthusiasm, I managed to convince them to allow me to tag along on their next field trip, hoping for a clue.

I wasn't to be disappointed.

Δ

I got what I came for when we were packing up to leave.

I noticed Fabien chatting with Bruno and Cédric, and ambled over to join them. Something compelled me; maybe it was their demeanour, or just some uncanny inkling.

Bruno was doing most of the talking. With his solid build, trimmed beard and dark, curly hair, he looked more like a fisherman than a volcanologist. Cédric, the tallest team member, and at twenty-four the youngest, was doing most of the nodding – his head was bouncing like a bobble toy.

'Maybe John has seen them,' Fabien said when he

noticed me, switching the conversation, once again, to English.

'Seen who?' I asked.

'The Russians.'

'Russians?'

'Sure. Have you noticed a group of Russians around the town? Around Goma?'

'I don't think so. Why?'

'Well we were just talking about them, and we think they are mercenaries.'

'Because they're Russian?'

'Maybe, but when you see them... maybe you will think so too. It is a fact that Russian mercenaries are helping the rebels, the... anti-government militia.'

Bruno and Cédric were looking at me, with Cédric nodding his agreement.

'Russian, huh,' I said, nodding back. 'Right. But no, I don't think I've seen them—'

'It was *your* hotel, where we...?' Fabien said to Bruno, but then went on, 'Oh no, it was Virginie and Thierry's.' The team's worst-kept secret seemed to be that Virginie and Thierry were an item.

'Virginie!' Fabien shouted out, at seeing her walking by. She altered course and joined us. Virginie was slim and energetic, and had short, straight, mousey-coloured hair with one half dyed a flash of pink. If I hadn't been focussed on Dala, I suspect I would have fallen for Virginie.

'The Russians,' said Fabien, doggedly anchoring the

conversation to English, 'they were staying at your hotel, no?'

'Yes they were,' she said. 'Until around... a week ago.'

'And they looked like mercenaries to you?'

'*Mercenaires*?' She pondered the question for a moment. 'Maybe, yes. It is possible. Although we saw... I often saw a woman with them, a Westerner, so... I don't know.'

'Speaking in Russian?'

'I think, yes, but maybe also in French as well.'

'But not in English?'

'No.'

I had a funny feeling about this. Could it have been Dala? I asked Virginie what she looked like, this mystery woman.

'Around my height,' she said. 'Very... brown. Tanned.'

'And her hair?

'I'm not sure. Dark? She always wore a cap, I think, so...'

I wondered if I should show her the photograph. Up until now, I'd resisted showing it to anyone on the team, in case it raised their suspicions about me. But now, I decided I had to.

'Can I show you something?' The others looked on as I rummaged about in my bag before producing the photo. It was the same photo I'd been carrying with me since that fateful day in Geneva. Needless to say, it was slightly the worse for wear – a bit like me. 'Could this be the woman?'

'I'm not sure,' Virginie said, but kept looking at it. 'Actually you know... Yes. It does look like her.' I don't know if my heart missed a beat, but for a moment I couldn't breathe. 'I'm not sure about the hair, and her eyes, I don't remember such remarkable eyes, *blue* eyes. I didn't notice their colour I suppose, but yes. It could be her.' She then looked up and spotted Thierry chatting to Nicolas nearby. 'Hold on, Thierry might know. You don't mind if I show him this?'

While Virginie was showing Thierry the photo, I noticed Fabien looking at me strangely.

'So are you a cop, or a bounty hunter or something?' he said.

'God no. Not at all. No, it's just that this woman, who's French, she's a friend... or rather, a friend of a friend's... and it seems she could be in some kind of trouble. She went missing in Rwanda a month ago, so I told her friend... who's *my* friend... that I'd, you know, keep an eye out for her. Make some enquiries.'

Fabien nodded, but continued to look at me dubiously as Virginie returned.

'Like me, he's not sure,' she said, 'but he agrees it could be her. Who is she?'

'Just a friend,' I said, avoiding Fabien's quizzical gaze, 'but which hotel are you staying at, if you don't mind me asking?'

'The Ihusi Hotel. It's on the lake.'

I couldn't get there fast enough, but kept my impatience to myself: I thoughtfully nodded my head and, in silence, suffered the agonizingly long time it took for the team to finish packing up, descend the mountain and drive into

Goma. As we didn't get back until late that evening, I had to wait until the next day before I was able get to the Ihusi Hotel in the Quartier des Volcans.

14.

SHE WAS either here, or had been here.

It wasn't just a feeling, it was something closer to knowledge. I was standing at the front entrance of the Ihusi Hotel on the morning after our return from Nyiragongo. On my way to the hotel, walking through the dusty streets, many of them unpaved, but always colourful – the people's clothes, the buildings, so much burnt orange and jewel blue – and taking in the contrast of smells – fresh fruit and rotting vegetables, flowers and sulphur – I once again took to seeing Dala everywhere. Every white tourist in the crowds of locals, everyone in my peripheral vision, every one of them was Dala. And now, looking up at the hotel signage, there was no doubt in my mind: she was here. Or had been.

I made my way through the hotel grounds, past the

lakeside swimming pool and up to reception. It was modern and fresh: black marble floor, polished to a mirrored perfection, and clean, coral-pink walls. The man behind the counter, who was wearing a crisp, brilliant-white shirt beneath his ash-grey hotel vest, had a bald head as black and shiny as the floors. Over the doorway, a wall-mounted TV was offering up the news, most of it, as usual, bleak.

He looked like a man who didn't do pleasantries, so I cut to the chase and showed him the photo of Dala.

'I'm trying to find a friend of mine,' I said in French, 'and I was wondering if you might have seen her.'

The man stared at the photo for a moment and then dipped his head to one side indicating he *might* have seen her. He remained mute.

'I understand she was here, not so long ago,' I added.

Still nothing.

'Last week, I'm told.'

He dipped his head again and smiled at me. 'I'm not sure, sir.'

'Listen,' I said. 'This is extremely important.'

I pulled out a pre-prepared wad of Congolese francs, about twenty US dollars' worth and laid it down on the counter between us.

The man looked at the wad of notes as if it were a dead rat and gave me a bemused shrug, before adding apologetically: 'I'm *really* not sure, sir.'

I produced a US twenty-dollar bill and swapped it for the Congolese francs. 'Anything you can remember... anything at all... would be helpful.'

He stared for a moment at the banknote with its picture of the White House, looked around to make sure no-one was watching and then slipped it into the top pocket of his beautifully laundered shirt. He smiled at me again. 'The more I think about it,' he said, 'yes. There *was* a woman who looked like her.'

'Last week?'

He nodded.

'Staying here? In the hotel?'

He stared at me for a few seconds. 'I am very sorry sir, but it would be against the law for me to give out information about the guests.'

'About the guests. So she *was* staying. Under what name?'

He resolutely shook his head.

'I absolutely cannot say, sir. Not for all the money in Africa.'

I put down another twenty-dollar bill. The man's eyes barely left mine as he clocked the note in an eyeblink and then continued to look at me with his Mona Lisa smile. When I added a further twenty dollars, he quickly but casually scooped up the two notes and turned his attention to the hotel register on his computer screen. He tapped a few keys.

'Her name was… Dominique Pin,' he said, not looking up.

'Dominique…?'

'Pin. P. I. N.'

Δ

I wondered then – as I wonder now – whether Dala chose the surname Pin for its similarity to my own, Penne, or possibly to the Île des Pins, the Isle of Pines. Or both, perhaps. Was it a kind of tribute, or a toast, to me? Or to us? Some sort of celebration, or her own way of remembering? Or, more than that, was she attempting to send some sort of message to me on the assumption that I'd still be on her trail?

Or was I – and am I – just fooling myself?

Δ

'French passport,' the man added, still looking at his screen. 'She checked out on… Friday 21 October.'

'A week ago. Right. So let me ask, did you notice if she was hanging out with the Russians who were staying here?'

'I really don't know, sir. When I saw her she was on her own.'

'Was she with a man? Or did she have her own room?'

I held my breath while he double-checked the register.

'Her own room.'

'I see,' I said, trying not show the relief I was feeling. This relief, as foolish as it was, might have had something to do with what I said next. 'I don't suppose you have a room available?'

He did, as it turned out. Not for that night, but there was availability from the following day onwards, and I went ahead and booked. The knowledge that I would soon be staying in the same hotel as the one Dala had been staying in was, in no small way, gratifying.

'Do you remember anything else about her?' I asked as I was about to leave. 'Anything at all? About what she did?'

He was shaking his head. 'No sir, I'm sorry.'

'OK, well thank you. You've been exceptionally helpful.'

I turned to go, feeling a lightness I hadn't felt in months.

'Actually, there was one thing,' he said. 'The last time I saw her, she was asking questions about Mount Karisimbi.'

'Mount Karisimbi?'

The man nodded. 'Yes sir.'

'Did she say why?'

'No sir. I thought maybe for sightseeing, maybe to see the mountain gorillas… I have many contacts I could have given her… but she wasn't interested in booking a trek.'

'Not interested,' I said. I thought about this for a moment. 'Thank you.' I turned to go once again, but something occurred to me. 'You said you have many contacts. If I wanted to go to Mount Karisimbi myself, would you be able to organize a guide to go with me?'

'Certainly, sir. However, allow me to suggest you take more than just a guide. It is a dangerous area and a rigorous trek… it would be helpful for you to bring some porters. At least two.'

'OK. That's fine. How soon can I go?'

'Leave it with me, sir, I will find out. But please be aware it is not the usual hiking season, and you can only go if the weather is good. There may be a delay of a day or two.'

On my way out, I saw Virginie arriving with Thierry. The two volcanologist lovers. They didn't see me and I didn't see any reason to change that. They looked happy and I'd leave them to their happiness. Maybe there was some of that for me too, I thought. Waiting around the corner.

15.

Wednesday, 2 November
Mount Karisimbi,
Democratic Republic Of Congo

SHE DIDN'T leave footprints.

Despite the absence of telltale signs though, my spirits were high: I knew she was close. My faith was almost religious.

Actually, you can scratch the almost, my faith *was* religious. That's how things were, now. She was the closest thing I had – the closest thing I'd ever had – to a god.

Mount Karisimbi (elevation 4,507 m / 14,787 ft), the highest mountain in the region, is regarded as one of the world's most topographically prominent peaks, given the way it rises up so dramatically out of the surrounding landscape, and from a distance it presents an impressive sight, particularly when it's capped with a dusting of snow. (Snow, despite the fact that the equator is less than 200 kilometres to the north.) It's also a dormant volcano: there hasn't been an eruption since around 8,000 BC. It straddles the border between the DRC and Rwanda, and on our trek to the summit, the invisible frontier was never more than a few hundred metres away at most.

We were setting up camp on the western flank of the mountain's upper slopes, at an altitude of 3,600 metres. It was the end of the first day of a two-day trek. I was accompanied by my Congolese guide, Ernest – amiable but taciturn – and two silent porters who I rarely got to speak to directly and whose names I was never told. One of the porters was carrying a rifle and appeared to be doubling as our armed escort, albeit a patently low-powered one.

There was no snow but it was cold – it was the type that cut through your clothes, and I could feel it through my field jacket and hiking trousers. The cloud and fog, at least, had temporarily cleared away. Having passed the 3,000-metre mark, we were now high enough to expect to feel some effects of the altitude – mainly an odd, discombobulated feeling in my case, along with some shortness of breath – and I stopped what I was doing for a moment to sit down and admire the view.

Perhaps my brain was affected by the altitude, but the view was so majestic it was transcendental.

The slope before me, with its low, alpine vegetation, quickly fell away, and opened out to a vast and undulating, green expanse of wayward forests and chequered fields. And volcanoes. The nearest, Mount Nyiragongo, whose steam-crowned crater rim I'd stood on only five days earlier, was only about twenty kilometres away, directly in front of me, and a still-potent, ruby-red sun was setting just to its left, its rays bathing us in a pink light. Further over and barely visible in the haze was Goma and Lake Kivu.

No longer visible was our four-wheel drive, which we'd left earlier that day. It was parked about fourteen hundred metres below us, in a dusty clearing at the edge of the forest – around seven kilometres away as the crow flies.

The purpose of the trek was to get a feel for the area generally, and to follow up on my best two leads so far: that Dala was somehow associated with Russian mercenaries operating in the region, and that she'd been asking questions about the mountain we were on, Mount Karisimbi. All I had to do was keep my eyes open.

And as I sat there, doing just that, and staring out at the poetic immensity before me, I had the inescapable feeling that something momentous was about to happen.

The immediate plan was to spend the night where we were, head off around 4am and make it to the summit just after sunrise, before trekking back down to our vehicle and returning to Goma. We'd be safely back by nightfall. That was assuming nothing cropped up. The whole point of the exercise, of course, was that something *might* crop up, and Ernest had already agreed the trek could be extended should the need arise. Obviously I, for one, was fervently praying that something *would* crop up.

Which just goes to prove the wisdom of the age-old warning to be careful what you wish for.

16.

Thursday, 3 November
Mount Karisimbi,
Democratic Republic Of Congo

SHE SPOKE to me, but I don't know what she said.

I'd been dreaming of her when my alarm went off in the pre-dawn dark, and all I can remember is she was talking to me, but I couldn't hear her words. As if she was behind a thick pane of glass.

It was bitterly cold and a sharp wind was blowing when I stepped out of my tent into the high-mountain blackness. The quality of the night is different at altitude: there's a stronger sense of the infinite, an unnerving feeling that infinity itself is somehow closer.

Ernest and the two others were already packed up, and a short time later we were moving out. There was no moon, nor was there yet any hint of dawn in the sky, so torches were essential.

There was a strange mood pervading our little group when we set off. Ernest, in particular, was on edge. He claimed he'd heard gunshots in the middle of the night. I suggested it might have been hunters or poachers, but it had sounded like they were using automatic weapons, AK-47s. And anyway, he said, there was nothing to hunt this high up on the mountain. Nothing, that is, except for people.

The slope was steep – even though our indirect, slightly corkscrewing path to the summit made the walking easier – and our progress was tortoise-like. We were four slow-moving dinner plates of light, bobbing gradually heavenwards. The cold air stung. There was nothing to see in the black emptiness to our left, but a memory of the view from half a day earlier.

And then, finally, after about an hour, there was a faint lightening of the eastern sky, precursor to a fresh awakening of a continent of shadows. Our path had taken us from the west flank around to the northern one, and so we knew that we'd soon be seeing the sun itself, rampaging over the horizon into day.

And we did, but it wasn't all that we saw.

It must have been getting on towards 6am. The sun had only just burst forth over the distant line of hills to the east, and we'd stopped, at an altitude of about 4,300 metres, to admire the view. Which was when Ernest noticed something.

'What is that?' he said. (We spoke in French – unlike the volcanologists, Ernest felt no compulsion to practice his sketchy English on me.) He was pointing, his hand shading his eyes. 'There's something there.'

At first I couldn't see what he was looking at. And then, when I moved closer to him, I saw it. An orange glint. A random ray from the rising sun was reflecting off something. Whatever that something was, it looked to be about a hundred metres away, ahead and up the slope from where we were standing. It was impossible to identify it with the naked eye, so Ernest pulled out his binoculars and looked through them, adjusting the focus wheel.

'It looks...' he said finally, his voice filled with uncertainty. 'I think... it is a man.'

'What's he doing?'

'Nothing,' Ernest said after a pause. 'He is on his back.'

'Is he dead?'

Ernest didn't reply but it was obvious what had to be done, and we wordlessly gathered up our packs and set off to investigate. It required taking a steeper line up the mountain than we otherwise would have, and my legs felt it.

As we closed in, what we were approaching gradually became clearer.

At one point I looked up and I could see, up ahead of us, the motionless body of a man – possibly a soldier – bathed in the deep-orange dawn rays like a stage actor in a spotlight. The body appeared to be shimmering, iridescent, and there was something almost portentous about the spectacle. As if we were not just seeing it, but beholding it.

We approached this ominous vision tentatively. Or at least Ernest and I did – the two porters stood back looking uncomfortable and anxious.

Up close, there was no doubt it was a soldier, nor that he was dead. His lifeless eyes were wide open and staring into the bright distance, and he was lying on his back with a bullet wound to his chest, advertised by a dark patch of blood on his jacket.

'What type of uniform is that?' I asked. It looked to be a fairly standard green and brown jungle fatigue, and with no obvious identifying marks.

'Not government,' Ernest said. 'He is from one of the rebel groups.' He looked up and surveyed the area. He pointed to the east. 'Just there. About twenty metres away. That is the border. That is Rwanda.'

'So we're still in the DRC here?' I asked and he nodded. I wasn't sure of the significance of this, except I presumed it had something to do with the soldier being a rebel.

There was a shout from behind us. It was the porter with the gun, pointing out spent bullet casings. Upon a closer inspection they were everywhere, showing through the foliage as little glimmers of gold.

'AK-47s,' said Ernest, examining one of them. And then he gave a hand signal to the porters to keep searching.

Even back then, I was familiar with the AK-47, or Kalashnikov. It's the most widely used firearm in the world, and that was why I'd been offered – and why I'd taken – a short course with the Service a few years earlier, covering the various aspects of its operation. I even got to fire one.

'Some sort of gunfight?' I said.

Ernest nodded. 'An ambush, probably. By national

soldiers. This was no doubt the shooting that I heard last night.'

I wanted to believe him. That government troops had been responsible. Because the thought had flashed across my mind: what if this was the work of Russian mercenaries? What if Dala was somehow connected to it? For obvious reasons, I sought a connection. That's why I was here, after all. But this wasn't the way I wanted to find her, associated with anything like this.

'So why here? Why all the way up here?

'Why not?' Despite his quick retort, Ernest pondered this for a moment, and continued. 'Some of these... militia groups... they operate out of camps in Rwanda. Apart from fighting the government troops in a battle for control of the region, they also traffic in diamonds and coltan. All of it, they smuggle it out of the country and into Rwanda. Then they sell it. The coltan they sell to China.'

I knew about coltan. The name is short for columbite-tantalite, and it's a metallic mineral that's a critical component of smart phones, computers and other electronic devices. In this part of the world, like 'blood diamonds', coltan is regarded as a 'conflict resource' due to the role it plays in funding the local rebel militias and prolonging civil war in the region. And the smuggled coltan does indeed end up in China and other East-Asian countries – with more than a little help from the multi-nationals who stand to profit by it.

'They were probably on the mountain,' Ernest continued,

'to avoid the main roads where there are military or police roadblocks.'

'Didn't help *him*,' I said, looking at the body.

'A patrol must have spotted them. To have found them, up here, in the middle of the night… they would have had to have been tipped off.'

But I wasn't really listening, because a strange feeling had overcome me, quite suddenly. It was almost overwhelming. I became frightened. I didn't know what was causing it, but assumed it was to do with the body, and being in the presence of violent death…

'Ernest!' One of the porters called out, and Ernest headed over to him to see what he'd found.

Despite my better judgement, I looked at the body again, more closely this time. I examined the soldier's face with his blank, lost stare.

He was young, more boy than man. Not a child soldier by any means, but it was a face that was boyish. Almost pretty.

I looked more closely again. *Oh my god*, I thought.

It's a woman.

And then, almost straight away…

The realisation hit me with the speed and power of a sudden physical force. It was as if I, too, had been shot through the heart. My legs felt weak and I made myself sit down. Before I crumpled.

Because the body, the soldier…

Dala.

And my worst nightmare began unfolding before my eyes.

It was clear why I hadn't recognized her earlier, and it wasn't just because of the uniform. Her hair was cut short, military-short, designed to look masculine. And what there was of it was now dyed jet black. Her blue-green eyes were now brown, presumably with the help of contact lenses. And her olive skin was now so tanned, it was almost as dark as a local's.

One last disguise, and her best.

'Mister John!'

It was Ernest. He was trying to get my attention about something, but I weakly raised a hand to indicate I needed a moment.

Because I'd just found out that SANDPIPER was dead. It was difficult to believe: that this migratory bird I'd been following across the globe for so long would be flying no more. The cognitive dissonance in my head was devastating: the impossibility of it, the incontrovertible truth of it.

I looked around, breathing deeply, tasting the air as if trying to find meaning in its composition. Or at least solace. But neither meaning nor solace was there to be found. The mountainside around us was steep and dotted with *dendrosenecio* trees or giant groundsel – primitive-looking plants, taller than a man, with stout candelabra branches topped with rosettes of thick green leaves. Collectively, they looked like a platoon of hostile invaders from another world.

Almost imperceptibly, the ground beneath us began to

shudder. It continued for a few moments, then stopped. You didn't need to be a volcanologist to realise it was unlikely to be Karisimbi's doing, waking up after a ten-thousand-year slumber, but you never knew, did you, and I started willing it to happen, aching to be blown into the sky and sucked down into the earth's fiery depths. The two of us, together. Dala and me. Melting and folding – *melding*, in unison – and then metamorphosing into solid stone, a single rock. A lustrous-black piece of obsidian. Or even better, a diamond. A sparkling diamond made up of the two of us, our atoms permanently frozen side by side, inseparably, inextricably united. Together forever.

'There are more bodies.' Ernest had returned, along with the two porters. 'Three. All from the same group, it looks like. It was definitely an ambush.'

With some effort, I forced myself to stand.

'This one...' I began. I was shocked at how faint and scratchy my voice sounded. 'It's a woman.'

'It is?' Ernest looked at her with wide eyes, as did the other two.

I nodded. 'I knew her.'

'Ohhh,' he said sympathetically, but asked no questions, perhaps out of tact.

I had questions, though. Many questions.

I bent down over Dala's body, intending to check her pockets.

One of the porters made a noise, and straight away Ernest chimed in:

'No, no. You shouldn't touch the body. It is bad luck. Especially as it is a woman.'

I wondered how much worse my luck could get. But I backed off, not really wanting to touch her anyway. Dreading the pain.

'We need to go,' Ernest said. I noticed the porters were nodding. 'It is not safe.'

'What we need to do…' I said slowly. 'She must have had a pack with her or something. We need to find her things. We need to… look for her things.'

'I didn't see anything. It is likely that there were others who escaped. They would have taken what they could. Any weapons or provisions.'

'Something may have been missed. It was dark. I don't believe there's nothing here. We have to keep looking.'

Ernest and the porters were patently unhappy about this, but shuffled off and continued searching all the same. I could tell how nervous they were, in the presence of the bodies, and in different circumstances I would have been as well. But I needed to know more. And I had a strong feeling there was something for me to find.

The truth of the matter is I was probably entertaining the notion that I'd find something relevant to me, to us – something that showed she was thinking of me. I think I was searching for some kind of proof that this thing with her had been *meaningful* in her eyes and not just mine. Evidence of a bond undiminished by time or distance. In my grief, I sought *assurance*.

I reflexively took in a sudden gulp of air. It happens at that altitude, you find yourself not breathing. You almost have to remember to keep doing it. Assuming that continuing to live is the plan.

I looked at Dala again. At the billowed bloodstain on her uniform – on the pocket over her once-beating heart. I knew I had to search her sooner or later, so I steeled myself and sat down again, next to her.

I leant over and began with the jacket pocket over her right breast.

It was an awful feeling, touching that dead body. That body, once so full of passion, something she had in common with the dormant volcano she died on. The instant I touched her, I realised it wasn't her anymore: she was now a mere body, an empty shell, and all I had left were memories.

Memories, like that first night together in the South Pacific. At the resort on the Isle of Pines. Dinner for two…

Δ

Our table was outside, lit by a candle and the light from a half-moon twinkling through the palm trees, and the sound of the booming ocean was rolling across the lagoon.

'You see the changing rooms over there by the pool?' Dala asked, after we'd finished eating.

I nodded.

'Meet you there in three minutes. Don't follow me, go via the garden.'

And with that she stood up and walked off, her dress

susurrating into the darkness.

I gave her a head start and then made my way towards the garden. With more than a degree of breathlessness, I followed its meandering path under the coconut palms, winding around koi-filled ponds and past ferns, hibiscus, wild orchids and frangipani trees, all lit by ankle-high garden lights. The path emerged in a dark clearing on the ocean side of the changing rooms, away from the bright lights of the pool area.

I circumnavigated the oval-shaped building until I came to an entrance. It was the female toilets, instantly reminding me of the incident at the station in Geneva.

A noise behind me, though, snatched me back to the present.

I could only just make out a figure on the beach, outlined against the dark waters of the lagoon.

'Dala?'

I walked towards her. The dimly lit white sand at the water's edge was pallidly reflected in her face. The water was gently lapping. There was giggling on the beach, in the distance.

'It's Jasmine,' she said.

Her shoulder straps were loose, and resting on the sides of her arms, and the top edge of her dress hung low, barely covering her breasts, barely resisting gravity. I stood there for a moment, my eyes continuing to accustom themselves to the gloom, and watched her blue-green eyes sparkle in the starlight. The way she looked at me, there was nothing that needed to be said.

In one movement she slipped out of her dress and walked, naked, across the narrow beach and into the sea. I did the same, flicking off my shoes and removing the rest of my clothes, and made my way over the cool sand and into the still-warm tropical waters.

Δ

And this was where memories would never be enough.

I remembered wading out to where she was standing, and I remembered our bodies touching, and her hand suddenly on me, and then my hand on her, and then in her, and her gasps, and her arching her back, and then I remembered how she suddenly pulled up, clutching my wrist and then with a sense of urgency took me by the hand and led me back to the beach, to where the grass met the sand, and in the darkness there, against the base of an upturned kayak, I remembered our naked bodies coming together in the open air for anyone to see, and her half-stifled cries for anyone to hear, and then, in the cool of the night, the explosions of pleasure. One thousand degrees hot.

Everything, now, a broken memory. And none of it enough.

'Mister John!!'

Ernest was hurrying towards me across the steep, uneven slope, stumbling and almost tripping over the rocks and clumps of grass. He held his binoculars in one hand, and was waving his other hand around to get my attention.

Meanwhile I'd finished my search of Dala's pockets and

found nothing. Maybe someone had got to her before me.

I considered trying to stand up, but thought better of it. My legs felt like lead.

Ernest was breathing heavily by the time he got to me and he had a pained look on his face.

'People coming,' he panted. 'In uniform. This is not good.'

'Where?'

He offered me his binoculars and pointed down the slope, but I was too dispirited to bother looking.

'We should move,' he said.

'How far away?'

'No more than half an hour.'

I couldn't have cared less whether it was half an hour or half a day.

'So?' I asked, although it was barely a question.

'This is not good. It's not good to stay here. Or…' And he pointed at Dala.

Or they might kill us too, he was implying. Which was fair enough, it was a reasonable point, but there was still work to be done.

'Keep looking.'

'But these people, they could be coming back. To retrieve the bodies.'

'We'll go when we find something. And no running away. Or no money, OK?'

It was harsh, but I was desperate. Or thought I was.

I forced myself to look over at Dala again, and I considered her uniform. Ernest had said it was the uniform of one of the rebel groups. Well, a rebel, she was certainly that, but a rebel soldier in the Congo? Fighting the government for control of the region and trafficking conflict resources?

'Mister John!' There is nothing here! Nothing at all!'

'Keep looking.'

So was this really the place she was 'swimming to', as she put it in that final note? Where they 'spoke her language'? But why here? And why a soldier?

I watched Ernest and the porters as they continued their half-hearted search around the dendrosenecios, snatching at blades of grass and occasionally looking up with wide eyes, appealing for me to see sense.

I thought about the last time I saw her. The last moment. Lunchtime, in the restaurant at the White Grass Ocean Resort on Tanna, Vanuatu. Dala had just told me about her upset stomach, and had stood up to leave. Unlike the evening before, there was no meaningful look. If anything she was impatient to get away, which at the time I'd put down to her not feeling well. But even though the moment was fleeting – I didn't even watch her walk out of the restaurant, didn't know I'd never see her alive again – it was enough to leave a snapshot in my head: framed for an instant by the blue Coral Sea in the background, my elusive mermaid.

Not that she was ever mine.

'They're police.'

It was Ernest. He was back, standing a couple of metres

down the slope from me, binoculars in hand and pointing. He was looking agitated, and shifting his weight from one leg to the other. I, of course, was still next to Dala, still sitting down, with no intention of getting up then, or for that matter, ever.

'The people coming,' he added, 'they're police from Goma.'

'Good. They can track down whoever did this.'

'Not good. They are not good people. Maybe they'll kill you.'

'The police? Why would they do that?'

Ernest looked at me for a moment, as if trying to decide whether to answer.

'For a while, the police used to protect the rebels in exchange for gold,' he said, 'but now the government pays the police lots of money and so instead of protecting the rebels they kill them.' He pointed to Dala's body. 'Maybe they'll say you are one of them. Maybe they'll put you in the same boat.'

The same boat as Dala. Funny. Ironic. Hadn't that been my goal?

Ernest went on:

'The police get paid so-called "bonuses" for making an extra effort to help protect against raids from Rwanda. Theft of coltan etcetera. They kill rebels and get paid per body. They take photos of the dead bodies as proof, and loot them as well.'

'Do all the police do this?'

'No. Not all. Most leave the rebels for the government soldiers to deal with, but still, there are some bad ones. Some very bad ones. And so if you're a rebel, and you're unlucky enough to be caught by the wrong type of police, they'll interrogate you and then kill you. They're brutal. They're worse than the soldiers. Because of the bonuses.'

'OK,' I said, trying a bit harder now to take all this in.

'Yes, OK? So you have to hope the police coming aren't the people who killed these rebels, but they probably are, and they're probably returning to take the photographs. And if they are, and catch us here, they'll assume we're friends of the rebels and kill us too. Please, we must not take any chances. We must leave *now*.'

Leaving, though, was not an option for me. Not yet. I was still tormented by the question of what Dala had been doing.

She'd been seen associating with Russian mercenaries, and it made sense that the mercenaries would be backing the rebels, but what was Dala doing with any of them in the first place? I doubted her involvement with the mercenaries had anything to do with her Russian ancestry. I also doubted her joining them, or the rebels, was simply some convoluted form of revenge against her own country, France. Or that she was helping the rebels at the behest of a foreign power for ideological reasons.

Was she simply seeking to enrich herself, like a true mercenary? Entirely plausible. And I had no doubt that what was also in play here was her professed desire to go to somewhere dangerous to 'cauterize the pain'. But even all that, I suspected, was only half the story.

The truth of it, I decided (and I still believe this), is that she was looking for something. And what was she looking for? Herself. Here, in the heart of Africa – immersed in all this explosive danger, where they 'spoke her language' – what she was really doing here was attempting to find herself.

And if that's what she was really doing, it occurred to me, what did that say about me? What if she was right and I was looking for myself in her? Where did that leave *me*? It felt a bit like looking in a double mirror.

I noticed that one of the porters was hurrying up the slope towards us. He was holding something in his hand.

'What is it?' I called out to him. I stood up, having finally found the energy. 'Have you found something?'

By the time he got to us, I could see that he was holding a black beret.

'You see?' Ernest said, after being handed the beret.

'What?'

'It's police. This is a police hat. A *Goma* police hat. Do you see now?' Ernest could see that I almost did, so he continued, endeavouring to make things clearer for me, all the while shaking the beret at me. 'It's a Goma police hat. Those people coming, they are *Goma* police.'

I got it. So certain members of the Goma police were probably the ones who killed the rebels, and in all likelihood, those same police were returning to photograph the bodies so they could get their bonuses. And here we were, with the bodies, getting in their way, messing up their day, and looking for all the world like the dead rebels' buddies.

Which, in at least one sense, was true.

'This is bad, very bad,' Ernest said. 'Mister John, we must go, this is very dangerous. Very, very dangerous.'

I knew he was right, and I should have listened to him. If we'd left then, and not stayed for as long as we did, the sequence of events that immediately followed would never have happened, and I almost certainly wouldn't have ended up where I am now.

But we didn't leave then. I didn't listen to my better judgement. Instead, I listened to whatever it was that had well and truly taken over my head, and as a consequence, I remained stubbornly determined to find something of Dala's. Anything. The retreating rebels may well have grabbed her pack and searched her pockets, but surely, I reasoned, in the night-time confusion, they had to have dropped something, missed something. And a wave of anger overcame me, and all I could think of was that I didn't travel this far to end up like this, on the side of a volcano in the middle of Africa, next to Dala's dead body, and without so much as a *single fucking clue*.

This was typical of Dala, I thought. Just her style, to leave me with nothing, just as she did the rest of the world.

'They must have seen us.' Ernest was looking through his binoculars. 'They are in a big hurry all of a sudden.'

'Stay down,' he added, now crouching next to me.

'Let me see.' I took the binoculars and sure enough there

they were, about six or seven of them in their blue uniforms and black berets, automatic weapons slung over their backs, scrambling up the slope. Still some distance away, but close enough. I handed the binoculars back.

'Get down!' implored Ernest. 'Don't let them identify you, they have binoculars too.'

I remained standing there though, staring at those tiny figures in the distance – and no doubt I stood there for too long – but I did so because something was niggling at me. Something to do with Dala leaving us all with nothing. And then it came to me.

'Please let's go. We must go.' Ernest was begging me now, desperate to get away.

'There's one more thing I have to check.'

Because I suddenly recalled what Dala had said about her favourite hiding place – her 'little secret', she'd called it – the best option for when you were travelling and not using airports: the heel of your shoe.

Her boots.

It didn't take long, although in my haste, I pulled her socks off along with her boots, exposing her bare feet, which I soon regretted. Ernest and the porters, needless to say, were completely baffled at this point, and beside themselves with anxiety. But I found what I was looking for soon enough: a compartment in the heel of her left boot, accessed through a miniature trapdoor in the insole.

And stuffed in there, wrapped in tissue, was a business card, along with two small stones. The stones were maybe a centimetre in diameter, pale and crystalline, and I was no expert but I'd seen my fair share of them by this stage and they looked to me like rough diamonds, straight from a mine. As for the business card, it bore the name of someone called Dmitry Egorov. There was also a Gmail address and a mobile number with a country code indicating it was Russian. My best guess was – and still is – that this was Dala's Russian connection, presumably one of the mercenaries or their organizer.

'Now! Please! Let's go! Please!' It was Ernest again. He was still crouching, but edging away, torn between his desire to be paid – or maybe it was loyalty – and fear. The poor guy was clearly panicked out of his brain.

'How close are they now?' Having just removed her boots, I was still sitting at Dala's feet – her dead, bare feet – and didn't have a clear view of the approaching figures.

'They're here!! They're here!! Let's go!!'

I slipped the card and the stones into my jacket pocket, and I stood up to better appraise the situation for myself.

'NO, NO, GET DOWN!!'

They were easy to spot. They were about a hundred metres away, down and around the mountain from us, possibly close to the spot where we ourselves had been when we'd first spotted Dala's body.

The sounds almost ran into each other, but there was an order to it: the first thing I heard was a *whiz* or zipping noise next to my ear, closely followed by a kind of flicking thud in the nearby tussock grass and then the distant whip-crack of a gunshot.

Which was when I realised they'd started shooting at us.

My first emotion was a rush of anger, and my first instinct, ridiculously, was to grab the porter's rifle and fire back. But I didn't – I wasn't suicidal – and sanity quickly prevailed, and as the zips and flicks and whip-cracks increased in frequency, and tufts of soil and vegetation erupted randomly around the four of us, there was nothing more that needed to be said and only one thing that needed to be done, and that's what we did. We ran.

We hurled ourselves down the mountain, leaving behind everything except what we were wearing. Out of the corner of my eye, I saw the porter with the gun throwing it away to lighten his load so he could run faster. He then flew past me, bounding over the vegetation like a gazelle.

Bullets were flying past me as well, still with their zipping and whizzing, and despite my lifelong atheism, I prayed for them to stop.

It was all a blur, but I just followed the others and tried to keep up. I believe at this point we were actually in Rwanda; not that it would have made a jot of difference, not with these people. I could tell, though, that Ernest was leading us down the slope at an angle, presumably to take advantage of the mountain's contours and eliminate the sightline between us and our attackers. It seemed to work – or my hypocritical prayer was answered – because all of a sudden the bullets stopped coming, and the last echo from the last gunshot crack quickly faded away. Nevertheless we weren't taking any chances, and we didn't stop running until we reached the cover of the forest. It was probably only a kilometre or two, but it felt like twenty.

To our great relief, they hadn't followed us. We suspected the police were more interested in the rebels' dead bodies than our, more elusive, live ones.

Now that we were among the trees, we were able to safely change direction, recross the border into the DRC, and cautiously make our way back to where we'd parked our four-wheel drive the previous morning. It was a long, tortuous slog – it took many hours – and all the while we were hoping the police wouldn't be there, at the end of it, to meet us.

Thankfully, they weren't.

17.

Thursday, 3 November
Ihusi Hotel, Goma,
Democratic Republic Of Congo

SHE'S GONE forever.

As I passed under the Ihusi Hotel sign over the entrance driveway, the only thought in my head was an impossible truth. This was in terrible, marked contrast to my first visit to the hotel, when a deep instinct told me she was near.

Ernest and the porters had just dropped me off. I'm sure they were pleased to be rid of me, but the sun was setting over Lake Kivu, the evening was mild, and it should have been a beautiful homecoming. Should have been, but for Dala.

The trip back had been uneventful, despite our fears of being arrested at a roadblock. I was exhausted, though, and must have looked a mess, after the long trek and our panicked scramble down the mountain, and all I could think of doing was showering and going to bed. Ideally never to wake up again.

My humble plan was soon to be foiled, however. Because as soon as I entered hotel reception, there they were. Two men in civilian clothes, looking out of place. As soon as they saw me, they approached me without hesitation and there were no prizes for guessing why.

Perhaps I knew they'd be there. Perhaps I no longer cared.

They showed me their police badges and it didn't take a genius to figure out what had happened. I'd been spotted on Mount Karisimbi (Ernest had tried to warn me). I was clearly a foreigner, so they didn't even need to worry about what vehicle we were in or set up roadblocks. All they had to do was ring around the major hotels and give them my description. The Ihusi Hotel was probably the first one they tried, too, given it was the hotel chosen by Dala and the Russians. Information about me booking the guide and porters was no doubt forthcoming. Money probably passed hands. Elementary.

The icing on the cake, from their point of view, was what they found in my jacket pocket: two rough diamonds and the business card of a suspected Russian mercenary coordinator.

18.

SHE SAW cruelty as simply a means to an end.

That was my assessment. Officer Kitenge was someone who'd clearly known great cruelty in her life – possibly committed against her, but certainly committed by her – and it struck me that she wasn't the type to employ it out of an emotional need. She saw it, rather, as a tool, and that was far worse. So my sole task, at this point, was to avoid being at the receiving end of it.

I'd spent the night in a cell at the back of the police station – if I was already looking somewhat dirty and dishevelled when I arrived back at the hotel, I was an even sadder sight now – and they were interrogating me in a room that was, at least, bigger than the one I'd slept in. AK-47s were carelessly scattered all over the place like tradesmen's tools.

Officer Kitenge was being not so ably assisted by Officer Mwepu, the one who'd lost his beret. *That* beret, I was willing to bet, the one we'd found on the mountain. Which was bad news for me, because it meant that these police were the same police that killed Dala and the rebels. Which meant they were the bad police that Ernest had told me about.

'So according to you, you are…'

Officer Kitenge was trying to read something. Presumably something with my name on it, maybe a poor copy of the hotel register. They obviously hadn't found my passport yet, although I wasn't sure why: it had been in the pack I'd abandoned near the summit of Mount Karisimbi, and you'd have thought they'd have discovered it by now. Possibly they assumed it belonged to one of the rebels. Possibly they assumed the passport was fake.

There was no point in telling her my name. I'd already told her I was a volcanologist (*je suis volcanologue*) and that I was British. Both assertions had been met with disbelief and great mirth, and there was no reason to think I'd be any more successful in convincing her that my name was really John Penne. Not that you could have blamed her.

The fact of the matter is, there was no point in telling her anything. I was already screwed.

She showed the piece of paper to Mwepu, who shrugged dully. No joy from the hotel register, obviously. She turned back to me and stared at my hair for a moment, then shook her head.

'You're from Moscow?'

'No. I told you. I'm British.'

'You are a mercenary, though.'

'No.'

'And you are from Russia.'

'No, I keep telling you, I'm—'

'Yes, yes, you keep telling me you're British.'

'Because I—'

'That's what you keep *saying*.'

'Because I *am* British.'

'And yet here you are speaking French.'

'Do you think no-one in the UK can speak French?' I said, immediately regretting it. Forgot that I was better off saying nothing.

There was an ugly pause.

'Do you think I'm stupid?' she asked aggressively.

I shook my head.

'Do you? You with your blond hair? And your...' She picked up a plastic evidence bag containing the two diamonds and the card, and shook it in my face. 'And your Russian friend's business card in your pocket? And your stolen diamonds? All of you staying in the same hotel? Do you think I'm some type of idiot who can't see what's up there written in big writing on the big wall? Do you take me for a fool? Do you?'

I said nothing.

'You're on Mount Karisimbi with the bodies of your dead friends... the same enemy fighters who tried to kill my people the night before... tried to kill *me*, tried to kill *Mwepu* here, tried to kill seven brave officers of the Goma police, *seven*… and you try to tell me you're there because you're a *volcanologist*?!'

I stayed silent.

'We don't *want* you Russians here!' she hissed at me. 'You kill our men and rape our women and steal our diamonds. Well no more. From now on, *we're* the ones doing the killing. From now on, *we* kill *you*.'

As I say, I was screwed.

19.

SHE WOULD have known what to do.

Dala would have found a way.

After my second night in the police station, I woke to a beautiful day that I was prohibited from sharing. I was nevertheless able to at least observe a small patch of it: a large, barred window in one of the four walls of my cell commanded a modest view of the sky. Today, it was a shining rectangle of brilliant blue.

The muffled noises of a busy Goma street, full of Saturday morning joy, found their way in through the glass: revving motorbikes, horns and excited shouts. If the window had been open, I might have been able to smell street food or incense. Even petrol fumes or livestock smells would have been welcome. Instead, I had to make do with a faint but inescapable odour of urine.

I wondered how long they intended to keep me in there. And what then.

The equation was a dismal one. If Ernest was to be believed, my chances of survival were low, given the reputation of my incarcerators and the damning evidence against me. And never mind that the picture painted by the evidence was a false one: the truth was no help to me either. An ex-MI6 spy chasing a fugitive French spy, how did that help exactly on a charge of being a mercenary? Not with police like these.

And it wasn't as if I could expect any help from the British government either. I wasn't allowed any communication with the outside world, and no-one knew I was here. Not that they'd necessarily help if they did. Given what had happened, they'd have every reason to cut me loose. It may have panned out differently if I'd still been with MI6, but I'd burnt that particular bridge long ago.

To put it simply, my position was hopeless.

Which made me think of Dala and wonder what she would have done. Of course I had no idea, because she wasn't here to ask, but then again, in a sense, maybe she was. Because when I thought about it, here we both were, in the Congo, with her dead on a mountainside and me as good as dead in the hands of her killers. And she would say I was here because I'd been trying to find myself in her. That being the case, and after spending so much time chasing her across the world, and so much effort attempting to put myself in her place, hadn't I now completed the transaction? Because hadn't I now just stepped into her shoes?

In a way, hadn't I now *become* her? Whoever she was?

20.

SHE'D HAD so many names, how could you hope to get a fix on someone like that?

Dala Gasnier, Chantal Fabre, Paola Leonetti, Jasmine Carroll, Dominique Pin: exactly whose shoes was I supposed to have stepped into?

Δ

It was two days later.

I'd just spent my fourth night in the cell with the single window. Soon I'd begin to lose track of time. But not yet. It was Monday. So why was I still there?

What were they waiting for? Had the executioner been away for the weekend? Had they run out of bullets and were trying to starve me to death? It wasn't like they were hanging out for a confession, intent on wearing me down to get there.

155

They'd already made up their minds what my story was, and as far as I could tell, they weren't impeded by anything that resembled a legal system. They weren't burdened with anything as tedious as a requirement to obtain a court order before taking matters a step further. So what was going on?

The ground shook.

And somewhere in the distance: a low, unnerving rumbling.

It wasn't the first time. These disturbances had begun the previous night and were becoming increasingly frequent. I guessed it was Mount Nyiragongo, gearing up again, ready for a fresh crack at Goma. In fact, as I was soon to learn, it was one of the other local volcanoes, Mount Nyamuragira – only thirty kilometres away and highly active – and this was the overture to its biggest eruption in a hundred years.

So now, it appeared, I had another tormentor.

My window to the world – which today, it being overcast, was a rectangle of grey – gave away few clues as to what was happening. I imagined the shouting in the street to be more urgent, but in truth there was probably little change.

I just had to hope there were no rivers of lava or pyroclastic surges headed our way. Or perhaps that was exactly what I had to hope for? Putting an end to this farce.

At least it gave me something else to think about – whoever this 'me' was.

Δ

How did I become this person, so unsure of myself and my identity, trying to find myself through others? Was it something in my childhood? Or was it always there, some latent, inalienable part of me?

I have an admission to make: John Penne isn't my real name.

Even though technically – legally – it *is* my real name, it's not the one I was born with. In truth, like Jeff Perry, it's just a construction. I ditched my birth name, changing it to John Penne, years ago, well before I joined the Service. Whether I did it as a form of rebellion, or out of a sense of melodrama, or for some other reason, I've never been completely sure.

At the time, there was no doubt in my mind: it was a rejection of my father, simple as that. But I didn't adopt my mother's surname either, and I changed not just my surname, but my first name too. So maybe it wasn't just about my father after all. Maybe it was some kind of search for an identity.

They say the only place to go looking when you're trying to find yourself is not a place you can travel to – it's not another country (or, it hardly needs saying, another person) – but rather it's inside you. It's *within* yourself.

But what if you peer in and find there's nothing there?

Δ

Later that morning, there was an unwelcome new development.

Ash.

At first, looking out my window to the world, it was barely perceptible against the grey vault of a sky. I perceived faint movement in the air, like drizzle or snow, but almost invisible, and thought my eyesight might be failing. But then, as it grew heavier, I realised that ash – volcanic ash – was falling from the heavens. Like a silent, grey blizzard, waves of it blew soundlessly against the windowpane. It deadened the already muted street sounds, although I could still hear enough to detect an increase in road traffic. People were leaving.

The earth tremors and the distant, rolling roars and rumbles – sounding like an approaching thunderstorm – were increasing in both intensity and frequency.

The chatter in the passageway outside my cell door was also increasing in magnitude. There were a series of shouts, although I couldn't make out what they were saying. A sense of general urgency pervaded the city, and the police station was clearly not immune.

Which is when the final unravelling began.

Or, to put it in the vernacular, it's where the shit started getting real.

It happened after a period of relative calm: the shouting had stopped, and so had the chatter – in fact for a few minutes, I couldn't hear any voices at all.

Then all of a sudden, the door to my cell burst open. An officer with a panicked look on his face – it was no-one I'd seen before – put his head in, said 'Oh sorry', and then he was gone again.

But he'd inadvertently left the door open.

I didn't give it a second thought. Which wasn't like me, not at all – it was as if I was possessed. I was certainly on a kind of autopilot. I slowly counted to ten, then quickly but coolly, and full of determination – or was it predetermination? – I walked out the door and closed it behind me.

I found myself in a corridor which had, to my right, at the far end, a door to the street, and to my left, access to the other cells and as far as I could see not much else. Counterintuitively, and to my own surprise, I found myself turning left. It felt like I was in a dream I was trying to make sense of.

I briskly moved down the corridor passing other closed cell doors. At the end, I came to an open doorway into the room where I'd been interrogated three days earlier. *Why am I going in here?* I asked myself as I entered the room.

I answered my own question when I observed myself picking up one of the AK-47s that I'd seen lying around the last time I was there. I chose one with a magazine attached. With my passable knowledge of AK-47s, I had no difficulty checking the magazine was fully loaded, and I then easily located the safety lever and pushed it down to the semi-auto position.

I walked back out of the interrogation room and headed back down the corridor towards the street exit. As I advanced along the narrow passageway, it soon became apparent that I would have to pass through an open-plan area where I'd be likely to find police officers at their desks. The logic of my earlier decision to head to the interrogation room began to make sense.

As I arrived at this open-plan area, I could see that the

exit door ahead of me was still a good fifteen metres away.

Looking to my left, I observed a cluttered space filled with unattended desks, overflowing rubbish bins and telephone books. A large, wide window let in light and revealed a darkening sky.

'Hey!'

With a strong sense of déjà vu, I turned – feeling as if I already knew what I was about to see – and there, to my right, standing behind a desk in the other half of the open-plan area, was Officer Kitenge. She was surrounded by more clutter: desks and bins, piles of paper and stacks of telephone books. And guns. There were guns, AKs, everywhere. Plus there was the revolver strapped to her hip.

As far as I could tell, Officer Kitenge was alone. Or if there was anyone else, they were making themselves scarce.

I saw her stare shift to the weapon I was holding securely in my two hands, pointed roughly in her direction.

I raised the AK and put the centre of her abdomen, her sternum, in my sights. Either I did it so quickly she had no time to move, or she froze, I can't say. I suspect the former.

Without hesitating, I pulled the trigger and fired off two shots, both of them hitting her in the chest, and throwing her backwards into the desk behind her. If the bullets hadn't killed her – which they almost certainly had – the force at which her head hit the concrete floor with a sickening crack would, without a doubt, have finished the job.

Had I done that out of necessity? Or was it revenge? And if it was revenge, on whose behalf? Dala's? Mine? Both?

When I walked over to make sure the policewoman wasn't moving, my attention was drawn to the desk she'd been standing at. On an impulse, I opened the top drawer and sitting there on a mess of paperwork was the plastic bag containing the diamonds and business card. I quickly grabbed it and shoved it into my trouser pocket.

Leaving Officer Kitenge behind, with her blood beginning to pool around her, I calmly continued on my way towards the door to the street. I'd barely recommenced my journey however, when Officer Mwepu entered through the street door, wearing, I couldn't help but notice, a new beret. He didn't see me straight away and I stopped where I was. Mwepu got all the way into the open-plan area, which I hadn't yet left – he was almost on top of me in other words – when he finally saw me.

I didn't need to point my gun. The mere sight of it was enough to make him freeze, as rooted to the spot as a dendrosenecio tree clinging to the slopes of Mount Karisimbi.

Eventually he raised his hands. I waved him off like you would a fly and he began to slowly walk backwards. He did a double take when he saw Kitenge's body, backed into a desk, tripped over a bin, spilling the contents everywhere, jumped up again and ran out of the room. It didn't escape my attention that, in the process, his new beret fell off. It made me wonder whether they only made police berets in the one size and Mwepu had a deceptively small head.

I turned and left the open-plan area, calmly strolled down the remaining fifteen metres or so of passageway, opened the door at the end and walked out into the street outside.

I was about to discard the gun I was still carrying, so as not to appear too conspicuous, but quickly realised I wouldn't have to.

Because outside it was chaos.

The sky was black. The ash was coming down heavily now, and the clogged streets were filled with people, cars and motorbikes, but mainly people, most of them on foot, leaving temporary tracks in the pervasive carpet of grey. Everyone had their mouths covered, and the usual vibrant colour of their clothes was lost in the ash-filled air, lending an underwater feeling to the whole scene. As with snow, the presence of the ash in the air and on the ground produced a muffling effect, as if someone had turned down the volume, or I had headphones on, and what should have been a cacophony of engine noise, whistles and shouting, was a subdued auditory sensation of movement, overlayed with the booms from the distant, waking volcano.

I took my jacket off and wrapped it around my neck and face, using it as a makeshift mask. I slung the AK-47 across my back and joined the surging crowd of people and machines.

I had escaped.

But where had I escaped to? Where was left for me to go?

There were options of course – there were always options – but for now I was happy to let these events play themselves out. After all, things were just starting to look up.

And anyway, something told me that one way or the other this story of mine was almost over.

Epilogue

I AM unrecognizable, even to myself.

It's not yet sunset, and there's already a cold wind hugging the ground and whistling through the bushes, even at this altitude, and I'm glad we're not camping any higher up. You'd think I'd be used to it by now, but some things you never really get used to.

It's been around six months since my escape from the police station in Goma and Nyamuragira's eruption. Goma came out of it all right in the end: the ash caused a few problems, killed some crops and livestock, and there was some property damage, but that was the extent of it. More bark than bite, you could say.

The way I see it, I came out of it all right too.

My appearance, however, has changed somewhat. After I got out of Goma – I ended up walking out on foot, the whole way, in that choking ash, a most unpleasant experience – I travelled up country for a bit. My light-coloured hair had become a serious hazard, and so I managed to get hold of some hair dye and cut my hair shorter and coloured it black.

And with no access to sunscreen, my skin colour is now several shades darker as well: I may not yet pass for an African, but I certainly wouldn't be readily mistaken for a European either. Possibly an Arab, or an Asian from the subcontinent.

One thing that hasn't changed: I still have the AK-47 that I stole from the police station slung across my back. It's always there, like an indispensable item of clothing.

Needless to say, I'm still on the run. Wanted for murder – the murder of a police officer – and an international warrant has been issued for my arrest. I assume they must have eventually found my passport. Good job.

Which goes some way to explaining what I'm doing with this outfit of rebel soldiers. When I left Goma, I was determined to go with the flow and allow things to unfold, and I did, and so here I am. We operate out of a base over the border in Rwanda, and we're currently in the middle of an operation. Smuggling diamonds and coltan, so no surprises there. The pay's not bad, it doesn't lack excitement as far as jobs go, and anyway, what else was I going to do?

Which reminds me: if it all suddenly goes pear-shaped, I've still got those two rough diamonds to help get me out of trouble, or at least tide me over. Safely hidden away in the heel of one of my boots. Along with the business card of Dmitry Egorov. I didn't need to call the number in the end – these guys I'm with were easy enough to find – but I hung onto the card, I'm not really sure why.

We're currently camped on the lower slopes of Mount

Karisimbi – the first time I've been back, in fact, since the trek with Ernest. I'm on guard duty, and I'm cold – *bloody* cold, with all this standing around – and I can't wait to get out of this wind and back to the warmth of the tents.

And back to the guys. They're a decent bunch. Mostly Rwandans, with a smattering of Congolese: there's Mamadou, Roland, Zeus, Joseph and Gautier, just to name a few. We even have a Russian: Ilya. Quiet. Keeps to himself. Super-friendly when you get a conversation going with him in his broken French, but touch his vodka and he'll kill you. Speaking of which, we originally had three Vlads, as the African guys call the Russians, but the other two weren't so lucky. If luck's the right word for it.

'Fabien!'

Someone's calling for me. It's Tonton, my replacement. About time. I wave back.

And yes, so, Fabien, that's me. I may be John Penne most of the time, but right now I'm Fabien Thibault. I did see fit to borrow the first name of my French volcanologist friend, and so now I'm French if anyone asks.

The new name's a necessity in my current circumstances, unfortunately. Perhaps it will become a long-term thing, and perhaps it will never be safe for me to use the name John Penne ever again.

No great loss I suppose, given I was never John Penne in the first place.

Δ

It's the middle of the night. There's a shout. Then gunfire. Then more shouting.

The camp is under attack.

At first I'm half asleep and I'm not sure what's going on. In my dream I was at a large garden party back in England, watching fireworks. When I wake up I switch on my torch and straight away a bullet passes within inches of my head, in one side of the tent and out the other, leaving two round holes. I douse the light immediately and get the hell out of there, grabbing my boots and jacket as I go.

It's a full-blown firefight. Our guys are firing back but it's clear we're heavily outgunned. I find some temporary cover behind a rock and put my boots and jacket on as fast as I can. I've stupidly left my gun back in the tent and it's too late to return there and get it. In fact it's too late to do anything useful because when I peer around the rock I can see the attackers' muzzle flashes and they're closing in.

They're using large spotlights: they're too large to be handheld torches, they're more like vehicle-mounted hunting lights, but I can't see any vehicles and we're too high up for vehicular access, so I can't figure it out and I don't have time to. There are beams of light and bullets flying everywhere and even though there are always options, right now I can only see one and it's the patch of darkness up the slope from where I'm crouching, so I make a run for it.

There's a slight ridgeline running up the mountain providing some limited cover, so I follow that.

The ridgeline, however, is too low, and every now and

then a beam of light catches me for an instant. The occasional zip and whiz of bullets remind me I haven't been forgotten. But I forge on up the mountain.

It's dark and cold, and the effort of running uphill at this altitude makes it feel like my lungs are about to burst, but I keep climbing, higher, and higher.

A fleeting thought occurs to me. It concerns Dala, and it's the first time I've thought of her in a while; I must have been pushing her away. But with a sudden clarity, the parallels become obvious. Because here I am, in rebel uniform, weaponless, on the upper slopes of Mount Karisimbi, my appearance darkened and changed beyond recognition, and with two rough diamonds and a Russian business card in the heel of my left boot. If anything were to happen to me now, if a bullet were to hit its mark, you'd hardly be able to tell us apart. If someone like me, say, were to come along the next morning and find me. Staring into the sunrise.

It's a striking thought, and at first it disorientates me. And then, for some reason, in this blur of an emergency, I find solace in it.

I press on.

I can see stars up ahead, beyond the summit. Beckoning me. And I have that feeling again, the same one I had the last time I was high up on this mountain at night: the powerful sense of the infinite, and the feeling that I'm closer to the edge of the universe.

I'm feeling something else, too. Despite the urgency and the danger, despite the cold, and my breathless desperation, and the burning in my legs and my lungs, and the beams of light that keep finding me and the persistent zipping of the bullets that refuse to leave me alone, and despite the fact that I could be dead and gone in an instant, forever beyond sensation and thought, I am strangely, inexplicably happy.

And then I have an overwhelming sense of it: for the first time in my life, I feel free. Truly – ecstatically – *free*.